C0-EDZ-653

# SARAH ORNE JEWETT

# The Queen's Twin and Other Stories

*The American Short Story Series*

VOLUME 66

GARRETT PRESS

512-00382-3

Library of Congress Catalog Card No. 69-11907

*This volume was reprinted from the 1899 edition
published by Houghton-Mifflin*
*First Garrett Press Edition published 1969*

*The American Short Story Series*
Volume 66
© 1969

Manufactured in the United States of America

GARRETT PRESS, INC.
*Publishers*
250 West 54th Street, New York, N.Y. 10019

To
SUSAN BURLEY CABOT

# CONTENTS

|  | PAGE |
|---|---|
| THE QUEEN'S TWIN | 1 |
| A DUNNET SHEPHERDESS | 38 |
| WHERE'S NORA | 73 |
| BOLD WORDS AT THE BRIDGE | 118 |
| MARTHA'S LADY | 135 |
| THE COON DOG | 170 |
| AUNT CYNTHY DALLETT | 195 |
| THE NIGHT BEFORE THANKSGIVING | 223 |

# THE QUEEN'S TWIN.

## I.

THE coast of Maine was in former years brought so near to foreign shores by its busy fleet of ships that among the older men and women one still finds a surprising proportion of travelers. Each seaward-stretching headland with its high-set houses, each island of a single farm, has sent its spies to view many a Land of Eshcol; one may see plain, contented old faces at the windows, whose eyes have looked at far-away ports and known the splendors of the Eastern world. They shame the easy voyager of the North Atlantic and the Mediterranean; they have rounded the Cape of Good Hope and braved the angry seas of Cape Horn in small wooden ships; they have brought up their hardy boys and girls on narrow decks; they were among the last of the Northmen's children to go adventuring to unknown shores. More than this one cannot give to a young State for its enlightenment; the sea captains and the captains' wives of Maine knew something of the wide world, and never mistook their native parishes for the whole instead of a part thereof; they knew not only Thomaston and Castine and Portland, but London and Bristol and Bordeaux, and the strange-mannered harbors of the China Sea.

One September day, when I was nearly at the end of a summer spent in a village called Dunnet Landing, on the Maine coast, my friend Mrs. Todd, in whose house I lived, came home from a long, solitary stroll in the wild pastures, with an eager look as if she were just starting on a hopeful quest instead of returning. She brought a little basket with blackberries enough for supper, and held it towards me so that I could see that there were also some late and surprising raspberries sprinkled on top, but she made no comment upon her wayfaring. I could tell plainly that she had something very important to say.

"You have n't brought home a leaf of anything," I ventured to this practiced herb-gatherer. "You were saying yesterday that the witch hazel might be in bloom."

"I dare say, dear," she answered in a lofty manner; "I ain't goin' to say it was n't; I ain't much concerned either way 'bout the facts o' witch hazel. Truth is, I 've been off visitin'; there's an old Indian footpath leadin' over towards the Back Shore through the great heron swamp that anybody can't travel over all summer. You have to seize your time some day just now, while the low ground's summer-dried as it is to-day, and before the fall rains set in. I never thought of it till I was out o' sight o' home, and I says to myself, 'To-day's the day, certain!' and stepped along smart as I could. Yes, I 've been visitin'. I did get into one spot that was wet underfoot before I noticed; you wait till I get me a pair o' dry woolen stockings, in case of cold, and I 'll come an' tell ye."

Mrs. Todd disappeared. I could see that something had deeply interested her. She might have fallen in with either the sea-serpent or the lost tribes of Israel, such was her air of mystery and satisfaction. She had been away since just before mid-morning, and as I sat waiting by my window I saw the last red glow of autumn sunshine flare along the gray rocks of the shore and leave them cold again, and touch the far sails of some coastwise schooners so that they stood like golden houses on the sea.

I was left to wonder longer than I liked. Mrs. Todd was making an evening fire and putting things in train for supper; presently she returned, still looking warm and cheerful after her long walk.

"There's a beautiful view from a hill over where I've been," she told me; "yes, there's a beautiful prospect of land and sea. You wouldn't discern the hill from any distance, but 't is the pretty situation of it that counts. I sat there a long spell, and I did wish for you. No, I didn't know a word about goin' when I set out this morning" (as if I had openly reproached her!); "I only felt one o' them travelin' fits comin' on, an' I ketched up my little basket; I didn't know but I might turn and come back time for dinner. I thought it wise to set out your luncheon for you in case I didn't. Hope you had all you wanted; yes, I hope you had enough."

"Oh, yes, indeed," said I. My landlady was always peculiarly bountiful in her supplies when she left me to fare for myself, as if she made a sort of peace-offering or affectionate apology.

"You know that hill with the old house right on top, over beyond the heron swamp? You'll excuse me for explainin'," Mrs. Todd began, " but you ain't so apt to strike inland as you be to go right along shore. You know that hill; there's a path leadin' right over to it that you have to look sharp to find nowadays; it belonged to the up-country Indians when they had to make a carry to the landing here to get to the out' islands. I've heard the old folks say that there used to be a place across a ledge where they'd worn a deep track with their moccasin feet, but I never could find it. 'T is so overgrown in some places that you keep losin' the path in the bushes and findin' it as you can; but it runs pretty straight considerin' the lay o' the land, and I keep my eye on the sun and the moss that grows one side o' the tree trunks. Some brook's been choked up and the swamp's bigger than it used to be. Yes; I did get in deep enough, one place!"

I showed the solicitude that I felt. Mrs. Todd was no longer young, and in spite of her strong, great frame and spirited behavior, I knew that certain ills were apt to seize upon her, and would end some day by leaving her lame and ailing.

"Don't you go to worryin' about me," she insisted, "settin' still's the only way the Evil One'll ever get the upper hand o' me. Keep me movin' enough, an' I'm twenty year old summer an' winter both. I don't know why 't is, but I've never happened to mention the one I've been to see. I don't know why I never happened to speak the name of Abby Martin, for I often give her a thought, but 't is a dreadful out-o'-the-way place where she lives, and I haven't seen her myself for three or four years. She's a real good interesting woman, and we're well acquainted; she's nigher mother's age than mine, but she's very young feeling. She made me a nice cup o' tea, and I don't know but I should have stopped all night if I could have got word to you not to worry."

Then there was a serious silence before Mrs. Todd spoke again to make a formal announcement.

"She is the Queen's Twin," and Mrs. Todd looked steadily to see how I might bear the great surprise.

"The Queen's Twin?" I repeated.

"Yes, she's come to feel a real interest in the Queen, and anybody can see how natural 't is. They were born the very same day, and you would be astonished to see what a number o' other things have corresponded. She was speaking o' some o' the facts to me to-day, an' you 'd think she 'd never done nothing but read history. I see how earnest she was about it as I never did before. I 've often and often heard her allude to the facts, but now she 's got to be old and the hurry 's over with her work, she 's come to live a good deal in her thoughts, as folks often do, and I tell you 't is a sight o' company for her. If you want to hear about Queen Victoria, why Mis' Abby Martin 'll tell you everything. And the prospect from that hill I spoke of is as beautiful as anything in this world; 't is worth while your goin' over to see her just for that."

"When can you go again?" I demanded eagerly.

"I should say to-morrow," answered Mrs. Todd; "yes, I should say to-morrow; but I expect 't would be better to take one day to rest, in between. I considered that question as I was comin' home, but I hurried so that there wa'n't much time to think. It 's a dreadful long way to go with a horse; you have to go 'most as far as the old Bowden place an' turn off to the left, a master long, rough road, and then you have to turn right round as soon as you get there if you mean to get home before nine o'clock at night. But to strike across country from here, there's plenty o' time in the shortest day, and you can have a good hour or two's visit beside; 't ain't but a very few miles, and it's pretty all the way along. There used to be a few good families over there, but they've died and scattered, so now she's far from neighbors. There, she really cried, she was so glad to see anybody comin'. You'll be amused to hear her talk about the Queen, but I thought twice or three times as I set there 't was about all the company she'd got."

"Could we go day after to-morrow?" I asked eagerly.

"'T would suit me exactly," said Mrs. Todd.

## II.

One can never be so certain of good New England weather as in the days when a long easterly storm has blown away the warm late-summer mists, and cooled the air so that however bright the sunshine is by day, the nights come nearer and nearer to frostiness. There was a cold freshness in the morning air when Mrs. Todd and I locked the house-door behind us; we took the key of the fields into our own hands that day, and put out across country as one puts out to sea. When we reached the top of the ridge behind the town it seemed as if we had anxiously passed the harbor bar and were comfortably in open sea at last.

"There, now!" proclaimed Mrs. Todd, taking a long breath, " now I do feel safe. It's just the weather that's liable to bring somebody to spend the day; I've had a feeling of Mis' Elder Caplin from North Point bein' close upon me ever since I waked up this mornin', an' I did n't want to be hampered with our present plans. She's a great hand to visit; she'll be spendin' the day somewhere from now till Thanksgivin', but there's plenty o' places at the Landin' where she goes, an' if I ain't there she'll just select another. I thought mother might be in, too, 't is so pleasant; but I run up the road to look off this mornin' before you was awake, and there was no sign o' the boat. If they had n't started by that time they would n't start, just as the tide is now; besides, I see a lot o' mackerel-men headin' Green Island way, and they 'll detain William. No, we 're safe now, an' if mother should be comin' in to-morrow we 'll have all this to tell her. She an' Mis' Abby Martin's very old friends."

We were walking down the long pasture slopes towards the dark woods and thickets of the low ground. They stretched away northward like an unbroken wilderness; the early mists still dulled much of the color and made the uplands beyond look like a very far-off country.

"It ain't so far as it looks from here," said my companion reassuringly, "but we 've got no time to spare either," and she hurried on, leading the way with a fine sort of spirit in her step; and presently we struck into the old Indian footpath, which could be plainly seen across the long-unploughed turf of the pastures, and followed it among the thick, low-growing spruces. There the ground was smooth and brown under foot, and the thin-stemmed trees held a dark and shadowy roof overhead. We walked a long way without speaking; sometimes we had to push aside the branches, and sometimes we walked in a broad aisle where the trees were larger. It was a solitary wood, birdless and beastless; there was not even a rabbit to be seen, or a crow high in air to break the silence.

"I don't believe the Queen ever saw such a lonesome trail as this," said Mrs. Todd, as if she followed the thoughts that were in my mind. Our visit to Mrs. Abby Martin seemed in some strange way to concern the high affairs of royalty. I had just been thinking of English landscapes, and of the solemn hills of Scotland with their lonely cottages and stone-walled sheepfolds, and the wandering flocks on high cloudy pastures. I had often been struck by the quick interest and familiar allusion to certain members of the royal house which one found in distant neighborhoods of New England; whether some old instincts of personal loyalty have survived all changes of time and national vicissitudes, or whether it is only that the Queen's own character and disposition have won friends for her so far away, it is impossible to tell. But to hear of a twin sister was the most surprising proof of intimacy of all, and I must confess that there was something remarkably exciting to the imagination in my morning walk. To think of being presented at Court in the usual way was for the moment quite commonplace.

### III.

Mrs. Todd was swinging her basket to and fro like a schoolgirl as she walked, and at this moment it slipped from her hand and rolled lightly along the ground as if there were nothing in it. I picked it up and gave it to her, whereupon she lifted the cover and looked in with anxiety.

" 'T is only a few little things, but I don't want to lose 'em," she explained humbly. " 'T was lucky you took the other basket if I was goin' to roll it round. Mis' Abby Martin complained o' lacking some pretty pink silk to finish one o' her little frames, an' I thought I 'd carry her some, and I had a bunch o' gold thread that had been in a box o' mine this twenty year. I never was one to do much fancy work, but we 're all liable to be swept away by fashion. And then there 's a small packet o' very choice herbs that I gave a good deal of attention to; they 'll smarten her up and give her the best of appetites, come spring. She was tellin' me that spring weather is very wiltin' an' tryin' to her, and she was beginnin' to dread it already. Mother's just the same way; if I could prevail on mother to take some o' these remedies in good season 't would make a world o' difference, but she gets all down hill before I have a chance to hear of it, and then William comes in to tell me, sighin' and bewailin', how feeble mother is. 'Why can't you remember 'bout them good herbs that I never let her be without?' I say to him — he does provoke me so; and then off he goes, sulky enough, down to his boat. Next thing I know, she comes in to go to meetin', wantin' to speak to everybody and feelin' like a girl. Mis' Martin's case is very much the same; but she's nobody to watch her. William's kind o' slow-moulded; but there, any William's better than none when you get to be Mis' Martin's age."

"Hadn't she any children?" I asked.

"Quite a number," replied Mrs. Todd grandly, "but some are gone and the rest are married and settled. She never was a great hand to go about visitin'. I don't know but Mis' Martin might be called a little peculiar. Even her own folks has to make company of her; she never slips in and lives right along with the rest as if 't was at home, even in her own children's houses. I heard one o' her sons' wives say once she 'd much rather have the Queen to spend the day if she could choose between the two, but I never thought Abby was so difficult as that. I used to love to have her come; she may have been sort o' ceremonious, but very pleasant and sprightly if you had sense enough to treat her her own way. I always think she 'd know just how to live with great folks, and feel easier 'long of them an' their ways. Her son's wife 's a great driver with farm-work, boards a great tableful o' men in hayin' time, an' feels right in her element. I don't say but she 's a good woman an' smart, but sort o' rough. Anybody that 's gentle-mannered an' precise like Mis' Martin would be a sort o' restraint.

"There 's all sorts o' folks in the country, same 's there is in the city," concluded Mrs. Todd gravely, and I as gravely agreed. The thick woods were behind us now, and the sun was shining clear overhead, the morning mists were gone, and a faint blue haze softened the distance; as we climbed the hill where we were to see the view, it seemed like a summer day. There was an old house on the height, facing southward, — a mere forsaken shell of an old house, with empty windows that looked like blind eyes. The frost-bitten grass grew close about it like brown fur, and there was a single crooked bough of lilac holding its green leaves close by the door.

"We'll just have a good piece of bread-an'-butter now," said the commander of the expedition, "and then we'll hang up the basket on some peg inside the house out o' the way o' the sheep, and have a han'some entertainment as we're comin' back. She'll be all through her little dinner when we get there, Mis' Martin will; but she'll want to make us some tea, an' we must have our visit an' be startin' back pretty soon after two. I don't want to cross all that low ground again after it's begun to grow chilly. An' it looks to me as if the clouds might begin to gather late in the afternoon."

Before us lay a splendid world of sea and shore. The autumn colors already brightened the landscape; and here and there at the edge of a dark tract of pointed firs stood a row of bright swamp-maples like scarlet flowers. The blue sea and the great tide inlets were untroubled by the lightest winds.

"Poor land, this is!" sighed Mrs. Todd as we sat down to rest on the worn doorstep. "I've known three good hard-workin' families that come here full o' hope an' pride and tried to make something o' this farm, but it beat 'em all. There's one small field that's excellent for potatoes if you let half of it rest every year; but the land's always hungry. Now, you see them little peakéd-topped spruces an' fir balsams comin' up over the hill all green an' hearty; they've got it all their own way! Seems sometimes as if wild Natur' got jealous over a certain spot, and wanted to do just as she'd a mind to. You'll see here; she'll do her own ploughin' an' harrowin' with frost an' wet, an' plant just what she wants and wait for her own crops. Man can't do nothin' with it, try as he may. I tell you those little trees means business!"

I looked down the slope, and felt as if we ourselves were likely to be surrounded and overcome if we lingered too long. There was a vigor of growth, a persistence and savagery about the sturdy little trees that put weak human nature at complete defiance. One felt a sudden pity for the men and women who had been worsted after a long fight in that lonely place; one felt a sudden fear of the unconquerable, immediate forces of Nature, as in the irresistible moment of a thunderstorm.

"I can recollect the time when folks were shy o' these woods we just come through," said Mrs. Todd seriously. "The men-folks themselves never'd venture into 'em alone; if their cattle got strayed they'd collect whoever they could get, and start off all together. They said a person was liable to get bewildered in there alone, and in old times folks had been lost. I expect there was considerable fear left over from the old Indian times, and the poor days o' witchcraft; anyway, I've seen bold men act kind o' timid. Some women o' the Asa Bowden family went out one afternoon berryin' when I was a girl, and got lost and was out all night; they found 'em middle o' the mornin' next day, not half a mile from home, scared most to death, an' sayin' they'd heard wolves and other beasts sufficient for a caravan. Poor creatur's! they'd strayed at last into a kind of low place amongst some alders, an' one of 'em was so overset she never got over it, an' went off in a sort o' slow decline. 'T was like them victims that drowns in a foot o' water; but their minds did suffer dreadful. Some folks is born afraid of the woods and all wild places, but I must say they 've always been like home to me."

I glanced at the resolute, confident face of my companion. Life was very strong in her, as if some force of Nature were personified in this simple-hearted woman and gave her cousinship to the ancient deities. She might have walked the primeval fields of Sicily; her strong gingham skirts might at that very moment bend the slender stalks of asphodel and be fragrant with trodden thyme, instead of the brown wind-brushed grass of New England and frost-bitten goldenrod. She was a great soul, was Mrs. Todd, and I her humble follower, as we went our way to visit the Queen's Twin, leaving the bright view of the sea behind us, and descending to a lower country-side through the dry pastures and fields.

The farms all wore a look of gathering age, though the settlement was, after all, so young. The fences were already fragile, and it seemed as if the first impulse of agriculture had soon spent itself without hope of renewal. The better houses were always those that had some hold upon the riches of the sea; a house that could not harbor a fishing-boat in some neighboring inlet was far from being sure of every-day comforts. The land alone was not enough to live upon in that stony region; it belonged by right to the forest, and to the forest it fast returned. From the top of the hill where we had been sitting we had seen prosperity in the dim distance, where the land was good and the sun shone upon fat barns, and where warm-looking houses with three or four chimneys apiece stood high on their solid ridge above the bay.

As we drew nearer to Mrs. Martin's it was sad to see what poor bushy fields, what thin and empty dwelling-places had been left by those who had chosen this disappointing part of the northern country for their home. We crossed the last field and came into a narrow rain-washed road, and Mrs. Todd looked eager and expectant and said that we were almost at our journey's end. "I do hope Mis' Martin 'll ask you into her best room where she keeps all the Queen's pictures. Yes, I think likely she will ask you; but 't ain't everybody she deems worthy to visit 'em, I can tell you!"

said Mrs. Todd warningly. "She's been collectin' 'em an' cuttin' 'em out o' newspapers an' magazines time out o' mind, and if she heard of anybody sailin' for an English port she'd contrive to get a little money to 'em and ask to have the last likeness there was. She's most covered her best-room wall now; she keeps that room shut up sacred as a meetin'-house! 'I won't say but I have my favorites amongst 'em,' she told me t'other day, 'but they're all beautiful to me as they can be!' And she's made some kind o' pretty little frames for 'em all — you know there's always a new fashion o' frames comin' round; first 't was shell-work, and then 't was pine-cones, and bead-work's had its day, and now she's much concerned with perforated cardboard worked with silk. I tell you that best room's a sight to see! But you mustn't look for anything elegant," continued Mrs. Todd, after a moment's reflection. "Mis' Martin's always been in very poor, strugglin' circumstances. She had ambition for her children, though they took right after their father an' had little for themselves; she wa'n't over an' above well married, however kind she may see fit to speak. She's been patient an' hard-workin' all her life, and always high above makin' mean complaints of other folks. I expect all this business about the Queen has buoyed her over many a shoal place in life. Yes, you might say that Abby 'd been a slave, but there ain't any slave but has some freedom."

## IV.

Presently I saw a low gray house standing on a grassy bank close to the road. The door was at the side, facing us, and a tangle of snowberry bushes and cinnamon roses grew to the level of the window-sills. On the doorstep stood a bent-shouldered, little old woman; there was an air of welcome and of unmistakable dignity about her.

"She sees us coming," exclaimed Mrs. Todd in an excited whisper. "There, I told her I might be over this way again if the weather held good, and if I came I 'd bring you. She said right off she 'd take great pleasure in havin' a visit from you; I was surprised, she 's usually so retirin'."

Even this reassurance did not quell a faint apprehension on our part; there was something distinctly formal in the occasion, and one felt that consciousness of inadequacy which is never easy for the humblest pride to bear. On the way I had torn my dress in an unexpected encounter with a little thornbush, and I could now imagine how it felt to be going to Court and forgetting one's feathers or her Court train.

The Queen's Twin was oblivious of such trifles; she stood waiting with a calm look until we came near enough to take her kind hand. She was a beautiful old woman, with clear eyes and a lovely quietness and genuineness of manner; there was not a trace of anything pretentious about her, or high-flown, as Mrs. Todd would say comprehensively. Beauty in age is rare enough in women who have spent their lives in the hard work of a farmhouse; but autumn-like and withered as this woman may have looked, her features had kept, or rather gained, a great refinement. She led us into her old kitchen and gave us seats, and took one of the little straight-backed chairs herself and sat a short distance away, as if she were giving audience to an ambassador. It seemed as if we should all be standing; you could not help feeling that the habits of her life were more ceremonious, but that for the moment she assumed the simplicities of the occasion.

Mrs. Todd was always Mrs. Todd, too great and self-possessed a soul for any occasion to ruffle. I admired her calmness, and presently the slow current of neighborhood talk carried one easily along; we spoke of the weather and the small adventures of the way, and then, as if I were after all not a stranger, our hostess turned almost affectionately to speak to me.

"The weather will be growing dark in London now. I expect that you 've been in London, dear?" she said.

"Oh, yes," I answered. "Only last year."

"It is a great many years since I was there, along in the forties," said Mrs. Martin. "'T was the only voyage I ever made; most of my neighbors have been great travelers. My brother was master of a vessel, and his wife usually sailed with him; but that year she had a young child more frail than the others, and she dreaded the care of it at sea. It happened that my brother got a chance for my husband to go as supercargo, being a good accountant, and came one day to urge him to take it; he was very ill-disposed to the sea, but he had met with losses, and I saw my own opportunity and persuaded them both to let me go too. In those days they didn't object to a woman's being aboard to wash and mend, the voyages were sometimes very long. And that was the way I come to see the Queen."

Mrs. Martin was looking straight in my eyes to see if I showed any genuine interest in the most interesting person in the world.

"Oh, I am very glad you saw the Queen," I hastened to say. "Mrs. Todd has told me that you and she were born the very same day."

"We were indeed, dear!" said Mrs. Martin, and she leaned back comfortably and smiled as she had not smiled before. Mrs. Todd gave a satisfied nod and glance, as if to say that things were going on as well as possible in this anxious moment.

"Yes," said Mrs. Martin again, drawing her chair a little nearer, "'t was a very remarkable thing; we were born the same day, and at exactly the same hour, after you allowed for all the difference in time. My father figured it out sea-fashion. Her Royal Majesty and I opened our eyes upon this world together; say what you may, 't is a bond between us."

Mrs. Todd assented with an air of triumph, and untied her hat-strings and threw them back over her shoulders with a gallant air.

"And I married a man by the name of Albert, just the same as she did, and all by chance, for I did n't get the news that she had an Albert too till a fortnight afterward; news was slower coming then than it is now. My first baby was a girl, and I called her Victoria after my mate; but the next one was a boy, and my husband wanted the right to name him, and took his own name and his brother Edward's, and pretty soon I saw in the paper that the little Prince o' Wales had been christened just the same. After that I made excuse to wait till I knew what she 'd named her children. I did n't want to break the chain, so I had an Alfred, and my darling Alice that I lost long before she lost hers, and there I stopped. If I 'd only had a dear daughter to stay at home with me, same 's her youngest one, I should have been so thankful! But if only one of us could have a little Beatrice, I 'm glad 't was the Queen; we 've both seen trouble, but she 's had the most care."

I asked Mrs. Martin if she lived alone all the year, and was told that she did except for a visit now and then from one of her grandchildren, "the only one that really likes to come an' stay quiet 'long o' grandma. She always says quick as she's through her schoolin' she's goin' to live with me all the time, but she's very pretty an' has taking ways," said Mrs. Martin, looking both proud and wistful, "so I can tell nothing at all about it! Yes, I've been alone most o' the time since my Albert was taken away, and that's a great many years; he had a long time o' failing and sickness first." (Mrs. Todd's foot gave an impatient scuff on the floor.) "An' I've always lived right here. I ain't like the Queen's Majesty, for this is the only palace I've got," said the dear old thing, smiling again. "I'm glad of it too, I don't like changing about, an' our stations in life are set very different. I don't require what the Queen does, but sometimes I've thought 't was left to me to do the plain things she don't have time for. I expect she's a beautiful housekeeper, nobody couldn't have done better in her high place, and she's been as good a mother as she's been a queen."

"I guess she has, Abby," agreed Mrs. Todd instantly. "How was it you happened to get such a good look at her? I meant to ask you again when I was here t' other day."

"Our ship was layin' in the Thames, right there above Wapping. We was dischargin' cargo, and under orders to clear as quick as we could for Bordeaux to take on an excellent freight o' French goods," explained Mrs. Martin eagerly. "I heard that the Queen was goin' to a great review of her army, and would drive out o' her Buckin'ham Palace about ten o'clock in the mornin', and I run aft to Albert, my husband, and brother Horace where they was standin' together by the hatchway, and told 'em they must one of 'em take me. They laughed, I was in such a hurry, and said they could n't go; and I found they meant it and got sort of impatient when I began to talk, and I was 'most broken-hearted; 't was all the reason I had for makin' that hard voyage. Albert could n't help often reproachin' me, for he did so resent the sea, an' I 'd known how 't would be before we sailed; but I 'd minded nothing all the way till then, and I just crep' back to my cabin an' begun to cry. They was disappointed about their ship's cook, an' I 'd cooked for fo'c's'le an' cabin myself all the way over; 't was dreadful hard work, specially in rough weather; we'd had head winds an' a six weeks' voyage. They'd acted sort of ashamed o' me when I pled so to go ashore, an' that hurt my feelin's most of all. But Albert come below pretty soon; I'd never given way so in my life, an' he begun to act frightened, and treated me gentle just as he did when we was goin' to be married, an' when I got over sobbin' he went on deck and saw Horace an' talked it over what they could do; they really had their duty to the vessel, and couldn't be spared that day. Horace was real good when he understood everything, and he come an' told me I'd more than worked my passage an' was goin' to do just as I liked now we was in port. He'd engaged a cook, too, that was comin' aboard that mornin', and he was goin' to send the ship's carpenter with me — a nice fellow from up Thomaston way; he'd gone to put on his ashore clothes as quick's he could. So then I got ready, and we started off in the small boat and rowed up river. I was afraid we were too late, but the tide was setting up very strong, and we landed an' left the boat to a keeper, and I run all the way up those great streets and across a park. 'T was a great day, with sights o' folks everywhere, but 't was just as if they was nothin' but wax images to me. I kep' askin' my way an' runnin' on, with the carpenter comin' after as best he could, and just as I worked to the front o' the crowd by the palace, the gates was flung open and out she came; all prancin' horses and shinin' gold, and in a beautiful carriage there she sat; 't was a moment o' heaven to me. I saw her plain, and she looked right at me so pleasant and happy, just as if she knew there was somethin' different between us from other folks."

There was a moment when the Queen's Twin could not go on and neither of her listeners could ask a question.

"Prince Albert was sitting right beside her in the carriage," she continued. "Oh, he was a beautiful man! Yes, dear, I saw 'em both together just as I see you now, and then she was gone out o' sight in another minute, and the common crowd was all spread over the place pushin' an' cheerin'. 'T was some kind o' holiday, an' the carpenter and I got separated, an' then I found him again after I did n't think I should, an' he was all for makin' a day of it, and goin' to show me all the sights; he'd been in London before, but I did n't want nothin' else, an' we went back through the streets down to the waterside an' took the boat. I remember I mended an old coat o' my Albert's as good as I could, sittin' on the quarter-deck in the sun all that afternoon, and 't was all as if I was livin' in a lovely dream. I don't know how to explain it, but there has n't been no friend I've felt so near to me ever since."

One could not say much — only listen. Mrs. Todd put in a discerning question now and then, and Mrs. Martin's eyes shone brighter and brighter as she talked. What a lovely gift of imagination and true affection was in this fond old heart! I looked about the plain New England kitchen, with its wood-smoked walls and homely braided rugs on the worn floor, and all its simple furnishings. The loud-ticking clock seemed to encourage us to speak; at the other side of the room was an early newspaper portrait of Her Majesty the Queen of Great Britain and Ireland. On a shelf below were some flowers in a little glass dish, as if they were put before a shrine.

"If I could have had more to read, I should have known 'most everything about her," said Mrs. Martin wistfully. "I've made the most of what I did have, and thought it over and over till it came clear. I sometimes seem to have her all my own, as if we'd lived right together. I've often walked out into the woods alone and told her what my troubles was, and it always seemed as if she told me 't was all right, an' we must have patience. I've got her beautiful book about the Highlands; 't was dear Mis' Todd here that found out about her printing it and got a copy for me, and it's been a treasure to my heart, just as if 't was written right to me. I always read it Sundays now, for my Sunday treat. Before that I used to have to imagine a good deal, but when I come to read her book, I knew what I expected was all true. We do think alike about so many things," said the Queen's Twin with affectionate certainty. "You see, there is something between us, being born just at the some time; 't is what they call a birthright. She's had great tasks put upon her, being the Queen, an' mine has been the humble lot; but she's done the best she could, nobody can say to the contrary, and

there's something between us; she's been
the great lesson I've had to live by. She's
been everything to me. An' when she had
her Jubilee, oh, how my heart was with
her!"

"There, 't would n't play the part in her
life it has in mine," said Mrs. Martin gener-
ously, in answer to something one of her
listeners had said. "Sometimes I think
now she's older, she might like to know
about us. When I think how few old
friends anybody has left at our age, I suppose it may be just the same with her as it
is with me; perhaps she would like to know
how we came into life together. But I've
had a great advantage in seeing her, an' I
can always fancy her goin' on, while she
don't know nothin' yet about me, except
she may feel my love stayin' her heart sometimes an' not know just where it comes from.
An' I dream about our being together out
in some pretty fields, young as ever we was,
and holdin' hands as we walk along. I'd
like to know if she ever has that dream too.
I used to have days when I made believe
she did know, an' was comin' to see me,"
confessed the speaker shyly, with a little
flush on her cheeks; "and I'd plan what

I could have nice for supper, and I was n't goin' to let anybody know she was here havin' a good rest, except I'd wish you, Almira Todd, or dear Mis' Blackett would happen in, for you'd know just how to talk with her. You see, she likes to be up in Scotland, right out in the wild country, better than she does anywhere else."

"I'd really love to take her out to see mother at Green Island," said Mrs. Todd with a sudden impulse.

"Oh, yes! I should love to have you," exclaimed Mrs. Martin, and then she began to speak in a lower tone. "One day I got thinkin' so about my dear Queen," she said, "an' livin' so in my thoughts, that I went to work an' got all ready for her, just as if she was really comin'. I never told this to a livin' soul before, but I feel you'll understand. I put my best fine sheets and blankets I spun an' wove myself on the bed, and I picked some pretty flowers and put 'em all round the house, an' I worked as hard an' happy as I could all day, and had as nice a supper ready as I could get, sort of telling myself a story all the time. She was comin' an' I was goin' to see her again, an' I kep' it up until nightfall; an' when I see the dark an' it come to me I was all alone, the dream left me, an' I sat down on the doorstep an' felt all foolish an' tired. An', if you'll believe it, I heard steps comin', an' an old cousin o' mine come wanderin' along, one I was apt to be shy of. She was n't all there, as folks used to say, but harmless enough and a kind of poor old talking body. And I went right to meet her when I first heard her call, 'stead o' hidin' as I sometimes did, an' she come in dreadful willin', an' we sat down to supper together; 't was a supper I should have had no heart to eat alone."

"I don't believe she ever had such a splendid time in her life as she did then. I heard her tell all about it afterwards," exclaimed Mrs. Todd compassionately. "There, now I hear all this it seems just as if the Queen might have known and could n't come herself, so she sent that poor old creatur' that was always in need!"

Mrs. Martin looked timidly at Mrs. Todd and then at me. "'T was childish o' me to go an' get supper," she confessed.

"I guess you wa'n't the first one to do that," said Mrs. Todd. "No, I guess you wa'n't the first one who's got supper that way, Abby," and then for a moment she could say no more.

Mrs. Todd and Mrs. Martin had moved their chairs a little so that they faced each other, and I, at one side, could see them both.

"No, you never told me o' that before, Abby," said Mrs. Todd gently. "Don't it show that for folks that have any fancy in 'em, such beautiful dreams is the real part o' life? But to most folks the common things that happens outside 'em is all in all."

Mrs. Martin did not appear to understand at first, strange to say, when the secret of her heart was put into words; then a glow of pleasure and comprehension shone upon her face. "Why, I believe you're right, Almira!" she said, and turned to me.

"Wouldn't you like to look at my pictures of the Queen?" she asked, and we rose and went into the best room.

## V.

The mid-day visit seemed very short; September hours are brief to match the shortening days. The great subject was dismissed for a while after our visit to the

Queen's pictures, and my companions spoke much of lesser persons until we drank the cup of tea which Mrs. Todd had foreseen. I happily remembered that the Queen herself is said to like a proper cup of tea, and this at once seemed to make her Majesty kindly join so remote and reverent a company. Mrs. Martin's thin cheeks took on a pretty color like a girl's. "Somehow I always have thought of her when I made it extra good," she said. "I 've got a real china cup that belonged to my grandmother, and I believe I shall call it hers now."

"Why don't you?" responded Mrs. Todd warmly, with a delightful smile.

Later they spoke of a promised visit which was to be made in the Indian summer to the Landing and Green Island, but I observed that Mrs. Todd presented the little parcel of dried herbs, with full directions, for a cure-all in the spring, as if there were no real chance of their meeting again first. As we looked back from the turn of the road the Queen's Twin was still standing on the doorstep watching us away, and Mrs. Todd stopped, and stood still for a moment before she waved her hand again.

"There 's one thing certain, dear," she

said to me with great discernment; "it ain't as if we left her all alone!"

Then we set out upon our long way home over the hill, where we lingered in the afternoon sunshine, and through the dark woods across the heron-swamp.

# A DUNNET SHEPHERDESS.

## I.

EARLY one morning at Dunnet Landing, as if it were still night, I waked, suddenly startled by a spirited conversation beneath my window. It was not one of Mrs. Todd's morning soliloquies; she was not addressing her plants and flowers in words of either praise or blame. Her voice was declamatory though perfectly good-humored, while the second voice, a man's, was of lower pitch and somewhat deprecating.

The sun was just above the sea, and struck straight across my room through a crack in the blind. It was a strange hour for the arrival of a guest, and still too soon for the general run of business, even in that tiny eastern haven where daybreak fisheries and early tides must often rule the day.

The man's voice suddenly declared itself to my sleepy ears. It was Mr. William Blackett's.

"Why, sister Almiry," he protested gently, "I don't need none o' your nostrums!"

"Pick me a small han'ful," she commanded. "No, no, a *small* han'ful, I said, — o' them large pennyr'yal sprigs! I go to all the trouble an' cossetin' of 'em just so as to have you ready to meet such occasions, an' last year, you may remember, you never stopped here at all the day you went up country. An' the frost come at last an' blacked it. I never saw any herb that so objected to gardin ground; might as well try to flourish mayflowers in a common front yard. There, you can come in now, an' set and eat what breakfast you've got patience for. I've found everything I want, an' I'll mash 'em up an' be all ready to put 'em on."

I heard such a pleading note of appeal as the speakers went round the corner of the house, and my curiosity was so demanding, that I dressed in haste, and joined my friends a little later, with two unnoticed excuses of the beauty of the morning, and the early mail boat. William's breakfast had been slighted; he had taken his cup of tea and merely pushed back the rest on the kitchen table. He was now sitting in a helpless condition by the side window, with one of his sister's purple calico aprons pinned close about his neck. Poor William was meekly submitting to being smeared, as to his countenance, with a most pungent and unattractive lotion of pennyroyal and other green herbs which had been hastily pounded and mixed with cream in the little white stone mortar.

I had to cast two or three straightforward looks at William to reassure myself that he really looked happy and expectant in spite of his melancholy circumstances, and was not being overtaken by retribution. The brother and sister seemed to be on delightful terms with each other for once, and there was something of cheerful anticipation in their morning talk. I was reminded of Medea's anointing Jason before the great episode of the iron bulls, but to-day William really could not be going up country to see a railroad for the first time. I knew this to be one of his great schemes, but he was not fitted to appear in public, or to front an observing world of strangers. As I appeared he essayed to rise, but Mrs. Todd pushed him back into the chair.

"Set where you be till it dries on," she insisted. "Land sakes, you'd think he'd get over bein' a boy some time or 'nother, gettin' along in years as he is. An' you'd think he'd seen full enough o' fish, but once a year he has to break loose like this, an' travel off way up back o' the Bowden place — far out o' my beat, 't is — an' go a trout fishin'!"

Her tone of amused scorn was so full of challenge that William changed color even under the green streaks.

"I want some change," he said, looking at me and not at her. "'T is the prettiest little shady brook you ever saw."

"If he ever fetched home more 'n a couple o' minnies, 't would seem worth while," Mrs. Todd concluded, putting a last dab of the mysterious compound so perilously near her brother's mouth that William flushed again and was silent.

A little later I witnessed his escape, when Mrs. Todd had taken the foolish risk of going down cellar. There was a horse and wagon outside the garden fence, and presently we stood where we could see him driving up the hill with thoughtless speed. Mrs. Todd said nothing, but watched him affectionately out of sight.

"It serves to keep the mosquitoes off," she said, and a moment later it occurred to my slow mind that she spoke of the pennyroyal lotion. "I don't know sometimes but William's kind of poetical," she continued, in her gentlest voice. "You'd think if anything could cure him of it, 't would be the fish business."

It was only twenty minutes past six on a summer morning, but we both sat down to rest as if the activities of the day were over. Mrs. Todd rocked gently for a time, and seemed to be lost, though not poorly, like Macbeth, in her thoughts. At last she resumed relations with her actual surroundings. "I shall now put my lobsters on. They'll make us a good supper," she announced. "Then I can let the fire out for all day; give it a holiday, same 's William. You can have a little one now, nice an' hot, if you ain't got all the breakfast you want. Yes, I'll put the lobsters on. William was very thoughtful to bring 'em over; William *is* thoughtful; if he only had a spark o' ambition, there be few could match him."

This unusual concession was afforded a sympathetic listener from the depths of the kitchen closet. Mrs. Todd was getting out her old iron lobster pot, and began to speak of prosaic affairs. I hoped that I should hear something more about her brother and their island life, and sat idly by the kitchen window looking at the morning glories that shaded it, believing that some flaw of wind might set Mrs. Todd's mind on its former course. Then it occurred to me that she had spoken about our supper rather than our dinner, and I guessed that she might have some great scheme before her for the day.

When I had loitered for some time and there was no further word about William, and at last I was conscious of receiving no attention whatever, I went away. It was something of a disappointment to find that she put no hindrance in the way of my usual morning affairs, of going up to the empty little white schoolhouse on the hill where I did my task of writing. I had been almost sure of a holiday when I discovered that Mrs. Todd was likely to take one herself; we had not been far afield to gather herbs and pleasures for many days now, but a little later she had silently vanished. I found my luncheon ready on the table in the little entry, wrapped in its shining old homespun napkin, and as if by way of special consolation, there was a stone bottle of Mrs. Todd's best spruce beer, with a long piece of cod line wound round it by which it could be lowered for coolness into the deep schoolhouse well.

I walked away with a dull supply of writing-paper and these provisions, feeling like a reluctant child who hopes to be called back at every step. There was no relenting voice to be heard, and when I reached the schoolhouse, I found that I had left an open window and a swinging shutter the day before, and the sea wind that blew at evening had fluttered my poor sheaf of papers all about the room.

So the day did not begin very well, and I began to recognize that it was one of the days when nothing could be done without company. The truth was that my heart had gone trouting with William, but it would have been too selfish to say a word even to one's self about spoiling his day. If there is one way above another of getting so close to nature that one simply is a piece of nature, following a primeval instinct with perfect self-forgetfulness and forgetting everything except the dreamy consciousness of pleasant freedom, it is to take the course of a shady trout brook. The dark pools and the sunny shallows beckon one on; the wedge of sky between the trees on either bank, the speaking, companioning noise of the water, the amazing importance of what one is doing, and the constant sense of life and beauty make a strange transformation of the quick hours. I had a sudden memory of all this, and another, and another. I could not get myself free from "fishing and wishing."

At that moment I heard the unusual sound of wheels, and I looked past the high-growing thicket of wild-roses and straggling sumach to see the white nose and meagre shape of the Caplin horse; then I saw William sitting in the open wagon, with a small expectant smile upon his face.

"I've got two lines," he said. "I was quite a piece up the road. I thought perhaps 't was so you'd feel like going."

There was enough excitement for most occasions in hearing William speak three sentences at once. Words seemed but vain to me at that bright moment. I stepped back from the schoolhouse window with a beating heart. The spruce-beer bottle was not yet in the well, and with that and my luncheon, and Pleasure at the helm, I went out into the happy world. The land breeze was blowing, and, as we turned away, I saw a flutter of white go past the window as I left the schoolhouse and my morning's work to their neglected fate.

## II.

One seldom gave way to a cruel impulse to look at an ancient seafaring William, but one felt as if he were a growing boy; I only hope that he felt much the same about me. He did not wear the fishing clothes that belonged to his sea-going life, but a strangely shaped old suit of tea-colored linen garments that might have been brought home years ago from Canton or Bombay. William had a peculiar way of giving silent assent when one spoke, but of answering your unspoken thoughts as if they reached him better than words. "I find them very easy," he said, frankly referring to the clothes. "Father had them in his old sea-chest."

The antique fashion, a quaint touch of foreign grace and even imagination about the cut were very pleasing; if ever Mr. William Blackett had faintly resembled an old beau, it was upon that day. He now appeared to feel as if everything had been explained between us, as if everything were quite understood; and we drove for some distance without finding it necessary to speak again about anything. At last, when it must have been a little past nine o'clock, he stopped the horse beside a small farmhouse, and nodded when I asked if I should get down from the wagon. "You can steer about northeast right across the pasture," he said, looking from under the eaves of his hat with an expectant smile. "I always leave the team here."

I helped to unfasten the harness, and William led the horse away to the barn. It was a poor-looking little place, and a forlorn woman looked at us through the window before she appeared at the door. I told her that Mr. Blackett and I came up from the Landing to go fishing. "He keeps a-comin', don't he?" she answered, with a funny little laugh, to which I was at a loss to find answer. When he joined us, I could not see that he took notice of her presence in any way, except to take an armful of dried salt fish from a corded stack in the back of the wagon which had been carefully covered with a piece of old sail. We had left a wake of their pungent flavor behind us all the way. I wondered what was going to become of the rest of them and some fresh lobsters which were also disclosed to view, but he laid the present gift on the doorstep without a word, and a few minutes later, when I looked back as we crossed the pasture, the fish were being carried into the house.

I could not see any signs of a trout brook until I came close upon it in the bushy pasture, and presently we struck into the low woods of straggling spruce and fir mixed into a tangle of swamp maples and alders which stretched away on either hand up and down stream. We found an open place in the pasture where some taller trees seemed to have been overlooked rather than spared. The sun was bright and hot by this time, and I sat down in the shade while William produced his lines and cut and trimmed us each a slender rod. I wondered where Mrs. Todd was spending the morning, and if later she would think that pirates had landed and captured me from the schoolhouse.

## III.

The brook was giving that live, persistent call to a listener that trout brooks always make ; it ran with a free, swift current even here, where it crossed an apparently level piece of land. I saw two unpromising, quick barbel chase each other upstream from bank to bank as we solemnly arranged our hooks and sinkers. I felt that William's glances changed from anxiety to relief when he found that I was used to such gear; perhaps he felt that we must stay together if I could not bait my own hook, but we parted happily, full of a pleasing sense of companionship.

William had pointed me up the brook, but I chose to go down, which was only fair because it was his day, though one likes as well to follow and see where a brook goes as to find one's way to the places it comes from, and its tiny springs and headwaters, and in this case trout were not to be considered. William's only real anxiety was lest I might suffer from mosquitoes. His own complexion was still strangely impaired by its defenses, but I kept forgetting it, and looking to see if we were treading fresh pennyroyal underfoot, so efficient was Mrs. Todd's remedy. I was conscious, after we parted, and I turned to see if he were already fishing, and saw him wave his hand gallantly as he went away, that our friendship had made a great gain.

The moment that I began to fish the brook, I had a sense of its emptiness; when my bait first touched the water and went lightly down the quick stream, I knew that there was nothing to lie in wait for it. It is the same certainty that comes when one knocks at the door of an empty house, a lack of answering consciousness and of possible response; it is quite different if there is any life within. But it was a lovely brook, and I went a long way through woods and breezy open pastures, and found a forsaken house and overgrown farm, and laid up many pleasures for future joy and remembrance. At the end of the morning I came back to our meeting-place hungry and without any fish. William was already waiting, and we did not mention the matter of trout. We ate our luncheons with good appetites, and William brought our two stone bottles of spruce beer from the deep place in the brook where he had left them to cool. Then we sat awhile longer in peace and quietness on the green banks.

As for William, he looked more boyish than ever, and kept a more remote and juvenile sort of silence. Once I wondered how he had come to be so curiously wrinkled, forgetting, absent-mindedly, to recognize the effects of time. He did not expect any one else to keep up a vain show of conversation, and so I was silent as well as he. I glanced at him now and then, but I watched the leaves tossing against the sky and the red cattle moving in the pasture. "I don't know 's we need head for home. It 's early yet," he said at last, and I was as startled as if one of the gray firs had spoken.

"I guess I 'll go up-along and ask after Thankful Hight's folks," he continued. "Mother 'd like to get word;" and I nodded a pleased assent.

## IV.

William led the way across the pasture, and I followed with a deep sense of pleased anticipation. I do not believe that my companion had expected me to make any objection, but I knew that he was gratified by the easy way that his plans for the day were being seconded. He gave a look at the sky to see if there were any portents, but the sky was frankly blue; even the doubtful morning haze had disappeared.

We went northward along a rough, clayey

road, across a bare-looking, sunburnt country full of tiresome long slopes where the sun was hot and bright, and I could not help observing the forlorn look of the farms. There was a great deal of pasture, but it looked deserted, and I wondered afresh why the people did not raise more sheep when that seemed the only possible use to make of their land. I said so to Mr. Blackett, who gave me a look of pleased surprise.

"That's what She always maintains," he said eagerly. "She's right about it, too; well, you'll see!" I was glad to find myself approved, but I had not the least idea whom he meant, and waited until he felt like speaking again.

A few minutes later we drove down a steep hill and entered a large tract of dark spruce woods. It was delightful to be sheltered from the afternoon sun, and when we had gone some distance in the shade, to my great pleasure William turned the horse's head toward some bars, which he let down, and I drove through into one of those narrow, still, sweet-scented by-ways which seem to be paths rather than roads. Often we had to put aside the heavy drooping branches which barred the way, and once, when a sharp twig struck William in the face, he announced with such spirit that somebody ought to go through there with an axe, that I felt unexpectedly guilty. So far as I now remember, this was William's only remark all the way through the woods to Thankful Hight's folks, but from time to time he pointed or nodded at something which I might have missed: a sleepy little owl snuggled into the bend of a branch, or a tall stalk of cardinal flowers where the sunlight came down at the edge of a small, bright piece of marsh. Many times, being used to the company of Mrs. Todd and other friends who were in the habit of talking, I came near making an idle remark to William, but I was for the most part happily preserved; to be with him only for a short time was to live on a different level, where thoughts served best because they were thoughts in common; the primary effect upon our minds of the simple things and beauties that we saw. Once when I caught sight of a lovely gay pigeon-woodpecker eyeing us curiously from a dead branch, and instinctively turned toward William, he gave an indulgent, comprehending nod which silenced me all the rest of the way. The wood-road was not a place for common noisy conversation; one would interrupt the birds and all the still little beasts that belonged there. But it was mortifying to find how strong the habit of idle speech may become in one's self. One need not always be saying something in this noisy world. I grew conscious of the difference between William's usual fashion of life and mine; for him there were long days of silence in a sea-going boat, and I could believe that he and his mother usually spoke very little because they so perfectly understood each other. There was something peculiarly unresponding about their quiet island in the sea, solidly fixed into the still foundations of the world, against whose rocky shores the sea beats and calls and is unanswered.

We were quite half an hour going through the woods; the horse's feet made no sound on the brown, soft track under the dark evergreens. I thought that we should come out at last into more pastures, but there was no half-wooded strip of land at the end; the high woods grew squarely against an old stone wall and a sunshiny open field, and we came out suddenly into broad daylight that startled us and even startled the horse, who might have been napping as he walked, like an old soldier. The field sloped up to a low unpainted house that faced the east. Behind it were long, frost-whitened ledges that made the hill, with strips of green turf and bushes between. It was the wildest, most Titanic sort of pasture country up there; there was a sort of daring in putting a frail wooden house before it, though it might have the homely field and honest woods to front against. You thought of the elements and even of possible volcanoes as you looked up the stony heights. Suddenly I saw that a region of what I had thought gray stones was slowly moving, as if the sun was making my eyesight unsteady.

"There's the sheep!" exclaimed William, pointing eagerly. "You see the sheep?" and sure enough, it was a great company of woolly backs, which seemed to have taken a mysterious protective resemblance to the ledges themselves. I could discover but little chance for pasturage on that high sun-burnt ridge, but the sheep were moving steadily in a satisfied way as they fed along the slopes and hollows.

"I never have seen half so many sheep as these, all summer long!" I cried with admiration.

"There ain't so many," answered William soberly. "It's a great sight. They do so well because they're shepherded, but you can't beat sense into some folks."

"You mean that somebody stays and watches them?" I asked.

"She observed years ago in her readin' that they don't turn out their flocks without protection anywhere but in the State o' Maine," returned William. "First thing that put it into her mind was a little old book mother's got; she read it one time when she come out to the Island. They call it the 'Shepherd o' Salisbury Plain.' 'T was n't the purpose o' the book to most, but when she read it, 'There, Mis' Blackett!' she said, 'that's where we've all lacked sense; our Bibles ought to have taught us that what sheep need is a shepherd.' You see most folks about here gave up sheep-raisin' years ago 'count o' the dogs. So she gave up school-teachin' and went out to tend her flock, and has shepherded ever since, an' done well."

For William, this approached an oration. He spoke with enthusiasm, and I shared the triumph of the moment. "There she is now!" he exclaimed, in a different tone, as the tall figure of a woman came following the flock and stood still on the ridge, looking toward us as if her eyes had been quick to see a strange object in the familiar emptiness of the field. William stood up in the wagon, and I thought he was going to call or wave his hand to her, but he sat down again more clumsily than if the wagon had made the familiar motion of a boat, and we drove on toward the house.

It was a most solitary place to live, — a place where one might think that a life could hide itself. The thick woods were between the farm and the main road, and as one looked up and down the country, there was no other house in sight.

"Potatoes look well," announced William. "The old folks used to say that there wa'n't no better land outdoors than the Hight field."

I found myself possessed of a surprising interest in the shepherdess, who stood far away in the hill pasture with her great flock, like a figure of Millet's, high against the sky.

## V.

Everything about the old farmhouse was clean and orderly, as if the green dooryard were not only swept, but dusted. I saw a flock of turkeys stepping off carefully at a distance, but there was not the usual untidy flock of hens about the place to make everything look in disarray. William helped me out of the wagon as carefully as if I had been his mother, and nodded toward the open door with a reassuring look at me; but I waited until he had tied the horse and could lead the way, himself. He took off his hat just as we were going in, and stopped for a moment to smooth his thin gray hair with his hand, by which I saw that we had an affair of some ceremony. We entered an old-fashioned country kitchen, the floor scrubbed into unevenness, and the doors well polished by the touch of hands. In a large chair facing the window there sat a masterful-looking old woman with the features of a warlike Roman emperor, emphasized by a bonnet-like black cap with a band of green ribbon. Her sceptre was a palm-leaf fan.

William crossed the room toward her, and bent his head close to her ear.

"Feelin' pretty well to-day, Mis' Hight?" he asked, with all the voice his narrow chest could muster.

"No, I ain't, William. Here I have to set," she answered coldly, but she gave an inquiring glance over his shoulder at me.

"This is the young lady who is stopping with Almiry this summer," he explained, and I approached as if to give the countersign. She offered her left hand with considerable dignity, but her expression never seemed to change for the better. A moment later she said that she was pleased to meet me, and I felt as if the worst were over. William must have felt some apprehension, while I was only ignorant, as we had come across the field. Our hostess was more than disapproving, she was forbidding; but I was not long in suspecting that she felt the natural resentment of a strong energy that has been defeated by illness and made the spoil of captivity.

"Mother well as usual since you was up last year?" and William replied by a series of cheerful nods. The mention of dear Mrs. Blackett was a help to any conversation.

"Been fishin', ashore," he explained, in a somewhat conciliatory voice. "Thought you'd like a few for winter," which explained at once the generous freight we had brought in the back of the wagon. I could see that the offering was no surprise, and that Mrs. Hight was interested.

"Well, I expect they're good as the last," she said, but did not even approach a smile. She kept a straight, discerning eye upon me.

"Give the lady a cheer," she admonished William, who hastened to place close by her side one of the straight-backed chairs that stood against the kitchen wall. Then he lingered for a moment like a timid boy. I could see that he wore a look of resolve, but he did not ask the permission for which he evidently waited.

"You can go search for Esther," she said, at the end of a long pause that became anxious for both her guests. "Esther'd like to see her;" and William in his pale nankeens disappeared with one light step and was off.

## VI.

"Don't speak too loud, it jars a person's head," directed Mrs. Hight plainly. "Clear an' distinct is what reaches me best. Any news to the Landin'?"

I was happily furnished with the particulars of a sudden death, and an engagement of marriage between a Caplin, a seafaring widower home from his voyage, and one of the younger Harrises; and now Mrs. Hight really smiled and settled herself in her chair. We exhausted one subject completely before we turned to the other. One of the returning turkeys took an unwarrantable liberty, and, mounting the doorstep, came in and walked about the kitchen without being observed by its strict owner; and the tin dipper slipped off its nail behind us and made an astonishing noise, and jar enough to reach Mrs. Hight's inner ear and make her turn her head to look at it; but we talked straight on. We came at last to understand each other upon such terms of friendship that she unbent her majestic port and complained to me as any poor old woman might of the hardships of her illness.

She had already fixed various dates upon the sad certainty of the year when she had the shock, which had left her perfectly helpless except for a clumsy left hand which fanned and gestured, and settled and resettled the folds of her dress, but could do no comfortable time-shortening work.

"Yes 'm, you can feel sure I use it what I can," she said severely. "'T was a long spell before I could let Esther go forth in the mornin' till she 'd got me up an' dressed me, but now she leaves things ready overnight and I get 'em as I want 'em with my light pair o' tongs, and I feel very able about helpin' myself to what I once did. Then when Esther returns, all she has to do is to push me out here into the kitchen. Some parts o' the year Esther stays out all night, them moonlight nights when the dogs are apt to be after the sheep, but she don't use herself as hard as she once had to. She's well able to hire somebody, Esther is, but there, you can't find no hired man that wants to git up before five o'clock nowadays; 't ain't as 't was in my time. They 're liable to fall asleep, too, and them moonlight nights she's so anxious she can't sleep, and out she goes. There's a kind of a fold, she calls it, up there in a sheltered spot, and she sleeps up in a little shed she's got, — built it herself for lambin' time and when the poor foolish creatur's gets hurt or anything. I've never seen it, but she says it's in a lovely spot and always pleasant in any weather. You see off, other side of the ridge, to the south'ard, where there's houses. I used to think some time I'd get up to see it again, and all them spots she lives in, but I sha'n't now. I'm beginnin' to go back; an' 't ain't surprisin'. I've kind of got used to disappointments," and the poor soul drew a deep sigh.

## VII.

It was long before we noticed the lapse of time; I not only told every circumstance known to me of recent events among the households of Mrs. Todd's neighborhood at the shore, but Mrs. Hight became more and more communicative on her part, and went carefully into the genealogical descent and personal experience of many acquaintances, until between us we had pretty nearly circumnavigated the globe and reached Dunnet Landing from an opposite direction to that in which we had started. It was long before my own interest began to flag; there was a flavor of the best sort in her definite and descriptive fashion of speech. It may be only a fancy of my own that in the sound and value of many words, with their lengthened vowels and doubled cadences, there is some faint survival on the Maine coast of the sound of English speech of Chaucer's time.

At last Mrs. Thankful Hight gave a suspicious look through the window.

"Where do you suppose they be?" she asked me. "Esther must ha' been off to the far edge o' everything. I doubt William ain't been able to find her; can't he hear their bells? His hearin' all right?"

William had heard some herons that morning which were beyond the reach of my own ears, and almost beyond eyesight in the upper skies, and I told her so. I was luckily preserved by some unconscious instinct from saying that we had seen the shepherdess so near as we crossed the field. Unless she had fled faster than Atalanta, William must have been but a few minutes in reaching her immediate neighborhood. I now discovered with a quick leap of amusement and delight in my heart that I had fallen upon a serious chapter of romance. The old woman looked suspiciously at me, and I made a dash to cover with a new piece of information; but she listened with lofty indifference, and soon interrupted my eager statements.

"Ain't William been gone some considerable time?" she demanded, and then in a milder tone: "The time has re'lly flown; I do enjoy havin' company. I set here alone a sight o' long days. Sheep is dreadful fools; I expect they heard a strange step, and set right off through bush an' brier, spite of all she could do. But William might have the sense to return, 'stead o' searchin' about. I want to inquire of him about his mother. What was you goin' to say? I guess you'll have time to relate it."

My powers of entertainment were on the ebb, but I doubled my diligence and we went on for another half-hour at least with banners flying, but still William did not reappear. Mrs. Hight frankly began to show fatigue.

"Somethin's happened, an' he's stopped to help her," groaned the old lady, in the middle of what I had found to tell her about a rumor of disaffection with the minister of a town I merely knew by name in the weekly newspaper to which Mrs. Todd subscribed. "You step to the door, dear, an' look if you can't see 'em." I promptly stepped, and once outside the house I looked anxiously in the direction which William had taken.

To my astonishment I saw all the sheep so near that I wonder we had not been aware in the house of every bleat and tinkle. And there, within a stone's-throw, on the first long gray ledge that showed above the juniper, were William and the shepherdess engaged in pleasant conversation. At first I was provoked and then amused, and a thrill of sympathy warmed my whole heart. They had seen me and risen as if by magic; I had a sense of being the messenger of Fate. One could almost hear their sighs of regret as I appeared; they must have passed a lovely afternoon. I hurried into the house with the reassuring news that they were not only in sight but perfectly safe, with all the sheep.

## VIII.

Mrs. Hight, like myself, was spent with conversation, and had ceased even the one activity of fanning herself. I brought a desired drink of water, and happily remembered some fruit that was left from my luncheon. She revived with splendid vigor, and told me the simple history of her later years since she had been smitten in the prime of her life by the stroke of paralysis, and her husband had died and left her alone with Esther and a mortgage on their farm. There was only one field of good land, but they owned a great region of sheep pasture and a little woodland. Esther had always been laughed at for her belief in sheep-raising when one by one their neighbors were giving up their flocks, and when everything had come to the point of despair she had raised all the money and bought all the sheep she could, insisting that Maine lambs were as good as any, and that there was a straight path by sea to Boston market. And by tending her flock herself she had managed to succeed; she had made money enough to pay off the mortgage five years ago, and now what they did not spend was safe in the bank. "It has been stubborn work, day and night, summer and winter, an' now she's beginnin' to get along in years," said the old mother sadly. "She's tended me 'long o' the sheep, an' she's been a good girl right along, but she ought to have been a teacher;" and Mrs. Hight sighed heavily and plied the fan again.

We heard voices, and William and Esther entered; they did not know that it was so late in the afternoon. William looked almost bold, and oddly like a happy young man rather than an ancient boy. As for Esther, she might have been Jeanne d'Arc returned to her sheep, touched with age and gray with the ashes of a great remembrance. She wore the simple look of sainthood and unfeigned devotion. My heart was moved by the sight of her plain sweet face, weather-worn and gentle in its looks, her thin figure in its close dress, and the strong hand that clasped a shepherd's staff, and I could only hold William in new reverence; this silent farmer-fisherman who knew, and he alone, the noble and patient heart that beat within her breast. I am not sure that they acknowledged even to themselves that they had always been lovers; they could not con-

sent to anything so definite or pronounced;
but they were happy in being together in
the world. Esther was untouched by the
fret and fury of life; she had lived in
sunshine and rain among her silly sheep,
and been refined instead of coarsened, while
her touching patience with a ramping old
mother, stung by the sense of defeat and
mourning her lost activities, had given back
a lovely self-possession, and habit of sweet
temper. I had seen enough of old Mrs.
Hight to know that nothing a sheep might
do could vex a person who was used to the
uncertainties and severities of her companionship.

## IX.

Mrs. Hight told her daughter at once
that she had enjoyed a beautiful call, and
got a great many new things to think of.
This was said so frankly in my hearing that
it gave a consciousness of high reward, and
I was indeed recompensed by the grateful
look in Esther's eyes. We did not speak
much together, but we understood each other.
For the poor old woman did not read, and
could not sew or knit with her helpless hand,
and they were far from any neighbors, while

her spirit was as eager in age as in youth, and expected even more from a disappointing world. She had lived to see the mortgage paid and money in the bank, and Esther's success acknowledged on every hand, and there were still a few pleasures left in life. William had his mother, and Esther had hers, and they had not seen each other for a year, though Mrs. Hight had spoken of a year's making no change in William even at his age. She must have been in the far eighties herself, but of a noble courage and persistence in the world she ruled from her stiff-backed rocking-chair.

William unloaded his gift of dried fish, each one chosen with perfect care, and Esther stood by, watching him, and then she walked across the field with us beside the wagon. I believed that I was the only one who knew their happy secret, and she blushed a little as we said good-by.

"I hope you ain't goin' to feel too tired, mother's so deaf; no, I hope you won't be tired," she said kindly, speaking as if she well knew what tiredness was. We could hear the neglected sheep bleating on the hill in the next moment's silence. Then she smiled at me, a smile of noble patience, of uncomprehended sacrifice, which I can never forget. There was all the remembrance of disappointed hopes, the hardships of winter, the loneliness of single-handedness in her look, but I understood, and I love to remember her worn face and her young blue eyes.

"Good-by, William," she said gently, and William said good-by, and gave her a quick glance, but he did not turn to look back, though I did, and waved my hand as she was putting up the bars behind us. Nor did he speak again until we had passed through the dark woods and were on our way homeward by the main road. The grave yearly visit had been changed from a hope into a happy memory.

"You can see the sea from the top of her pasture hill," said William at last.

"Can you?" I asked, with surprise.

"Yes, it's very high land; the ledges up there show very plain in clear weather from the top of our island, and there's a high upstandin' tree that makes a landmark for the fishin' grounds." And William gave a happy sigh.

When we had nearly reached the Landing, my companion looked over into the back of the wagon and saw that the piece of sailcloth was safe, with which he had covered the dried fish. "I wish we had got some trout," he said wistfully. "They always appease Almiry, and make her feel 't was worth while to go."

I stole a glance at William Blackett. We had not seen a solitary mosquito, but there was a dark stripe across his mild face, which might have been an old scar won long ago in battle.

# WHERE'S NORA?

## I.

"Where's Nora?"

The speaker was a small, serious-looking old Irishman, one of those Patricks who are almost never called Pat. He was well-dressed and formal, and wore an air of dignified authority.

"I don't know meself where's Nora then, so I don't," answered his companion. "The shild would n't stop for a sup o' breakfast before she'd go out to see the town, an' nobody's seen the l'aste smitch of her since. I might sweep the streets wit' a broom and I could n't find her."

"Maybe she's strayed beyand and gone losing in the strange place," suggested Mr. Quin, with an anxious glance. "Did n't none o' the folks go wit' her?"

"How would annybody be goin' an' she up an' away before there was a foot out o' bed in the house?" answered Mike Duffy impatiently. "'T was herself that caught sight of Nora stealin' out o' the door like a thief, an' meself getting me best sleep at the time. Herself had to sit up an' laugh in the bed and be plaguin' me wit' her tarkin'. 'Look at Nora!' says she. 'Where's Nora?' says I, wit' a great start. I thought something had happened the poor shild. 'Oh, go to slape, you fool!' says Mary Ann. ''Tis only four o'clock,' says she, 'an' that grasshopper greenhorn can't wait for broad day till she go out an' see the whole of Ameriky.' So I wint off to sleep again; the first bell was biginnin' on the mill, and I had an hour an' a piece, good, to meself after that before Mary Ann come scoldin'. I don't be sleepin' so well as some folks the first part of the night."

Mr. Patrick Quin ignored the interest of this autobiographical statement, and with a contemptuous shake of the head began to feel in his pocket for a pipe. Every one knew that Mike Duffy was a person much too fond of his ease, and that all the credit of their prosperity belonged to his hard-worked wife. She had reared a family of respectable sons and daughters, who were all settled and doing well for themselves, and now she was helping to bring out some nephews and nieces from the old country. She was proud to have been born a Quin; Patrick Quin was her brother and a man of consequence.

"'Deed, I'd like well to see the poor shild," said Patrick. "I'd no thought they'd land before the day or to-morrow mornin', or I'd have been over last night. I suppose she brought all the news from home?"

"The folks is all well, thanks be to God," proclaimed Mr. Duffy solemnly. "'T was late when she come; 't was on the quarter to nine she got here. There's been great deaths after the winther among the old folks. Old Peter Murphy's gone, she says, an' his brother that lived over by Ballycannon died the same week with him, and Dan Donahoe an' Corny Donahoe's lost their old aunt on the twelfth of March, that gave them her farm to take care of her before I came out. She was old then, too."

"Faix, it was time for the old lady, so it was," said Patrick Quin, with affectionate interest. "She'd be the oldest in the parish this tin years past."

"Nora said 't was a fine funeral; they'd three priests to her, and everything of the best. Nora was there herself and all our folks. The b'ys was very proud of her for being so old and respicted."

"Sure, Mary was an old woman, and I first coming out," repeated Patrick, with feeling. "I went up to her that Monday night, and I sailing on a Widnesday, an' she gave me her blessing and a present of five shillings. She said then she'd see me no more; 't was poor old Mary had the giving hand, God bless her and save her! I joked her that she'd soon be marrying and coming out to Ameriky like meself. 'No,' says she, 'I'm too old. I'll die here where I was born; this old farm is me one home o' the world, and I'll never be afther l'avin' it; 't is right enough for you young folks to go,' says she. I couldn't get my mouth open to answer her. 'T was meself that was very homesick in me inside, coming away from the old place, but I had great boldness before every one. 'T was old Mary saw the tears in me eyes then. 'Don't mind, Patsy,' says she; 'if you don't do well there, come back to it an' I'll be glad to take your folks in till you'll be afther getting started again.' She hadn't the money then she got afterward from her cousin in Dublin; 't was the kind heart of her spoke, an' meself being but a boy that was young to maintain himself, let alone a family. Thanks be to God, I've done well, afther all, but for me crooked leg. I does be dr'amin' of going home sometimes; 't is often yet I wake up wit' the smell o' the wet bushes in the mornin' when a man does be goin' to his work at home."

Mike Duffy looked at his brother-in-law with curiosity; the two men were sitting side by side before Mike's house on a bit of green bank between the sidewalk and the road. It was May, and the dandelions were blooming all about them, thick in the grass. Patrick Quin reached out and touched one of them with his stick. He was a lame man, and had worked as section hand for the railroad for many years, until the bad accident which forced him to retire on one of the company's rarely given pensions. He had prevented a great disaster on the road; those who knew him well always said that his position had never been equal to his ability, but the men who stood above him and the men who were below him held Patrick Quin at exactly the same estimate. He had limped along the road from the clean-looking little yellow house that he owned not far away on the river-bank, and his mind was upon his errand.

"I come over early to ask the shild would n't she come home wit' me an' ate her dinner," said Patrick. "Herself sent me; she's got a great wash the day, last week being so rainy, an' we niver got word of Nora being here till this morning, and then everybody had it that passed by, wondering what got us last night that we were n't there."

" 'T was on the quarter to nine she come," said Uncle Mike, taking up the narrative with importance. "Herself an' me had blown out the light, going to bed, when there come a scuttlin' at the door and I heard a bit of a laugh like the first bird in the morning" —

" 'Stop where you are, Bridget,' says I," continued Mr. Quin, without taking any notice, " 'an' I 'll take me third leg and walk over and bring Nora down to you.' Bridget's great for the news from home now, for all she was so sharp to be l'aving it."

"She brought me a fine present, and the mate of it for yourself," said Mike Duffy. "Two good thorn sticks for the two of us. They 're inside in the house."

"A thorn stick, indeed! Did she now?" exclaimed Patrick, with unusual delight. "The poor shild, did she do that now? I've thought manny's the time since I got me lameness how well I'd like one o' those old-fashioned thorn sticks. Me own is one o' them sticks a man 'd carry tin years and toss it into a brook at the ind an' not miss it."

"They're good thorn sticks, the both of them," said Mike complacently. "I don't know 'ill I bring 'em out before she comes."

"Is she a pritty slip of a gerrl, I d' know?" asked Patrick, with increased interest.

"She ain't, then," answered his companion frankly. "She does be thin as a young grasshopper, and she's red-headed, and she's freckled, too, from the sea, like all them young things comin' over; but she's got a pritty voice, like all her mother's folks, and a quick eye like a bird's. The old-country talk's fresh in her mouth, too, so it is; you'd think you were coming out o' mass some spring morning at home and hearing all the girls whin they'd be chatting and funning at the boys. I do be thinking she's a smart little girl, annyway; look at her off to see the town so early and not back yet, bad manners to her! She'll be wanting some clothes, I suppose; she's very old-fashioned looking; they does always be wanting new clothes, coming out," and Mike gave an ostentatious sigh and suggestive glance at his brother-in-law.

"'Deed, I'm willing to help her get a good start; ain't she me own sister's shild?" agreed Patrick Quin cheerfully. "We've been young ourselves, too. Well, then, 't is bad news of old Mary Donahoe bein' gone at the farm. I always thought if I'd go home how I'd go along the fields to get the great welcome from her. She was one that always liked to hear folks had done well," and he looked down at his comfortable, clean old clothes as if they but reminded him how poor a young fellow he had come away. "I'm very sorry afther Mary; she was a good 'oman, God save her!"

"Faix, it was time for her," insisted Mike, not without sympathy. "Were you afther wanting her to live forever, the poor soul? An' the shild said she'd the best funeral was ever in the parish of Dunkenny since she remimbered it. What could anny one ask more than that, and she r'aching such an age, the cr'atur'! Stop here awhile an' you'll hear all the tark from Nora; she told over to me all the folks that was there. Where has she gone wit' herself, I don't know? Mary Ann!" he turned his head toward the house and called in a loud, complaining tone; "where's Nora, annyway?"

"Here's Nora, then," a sweet girlish voice made unexpected reply, and a light young figure flitted from the sidewalk behind him and stood lower down on the green bank.

"What's wanting wit' Nora?" and she stooped quickly like a child to pick some of the dandelions as if she had found gold. She had a sprig of wild-cherry blossom in her dress, which she must have found a good way out in the country.

"Come now, and speak to Patrick Quin, your mother's own brother, that's waiting here for you all this time you've been running over the place," commanded Mr. Duffy, with some severity.

"An' is it me own Uncle Patsy, dear?" exclaimed Nora, with the sweetest brogue and most affectionate sincerity. "Oh, that me mother could see him too!" and she dropped on her knees beside the lame little man and kissed him, and knelt there looking at him with delight, holding his willing hand in both her own.

"An' ain't you got me mother's own looks, too? Oh, Uncle Patsy, is it yourself, dear? I often heard about you, and I brought you me mother's heart's love, 'deed I did then! It's many a lovely present of a pound you've sent us. An' I've got a thorn stick that grew in the hedge, goin' up the little rise of ground above the Wishin' Brook, sir; mother said you'd mind the place well when I told you."

"I do then, me shild," said Patrick Quin, with dignity; "'t is manny the day we all played there together, for all we're so scattered now and some dead, too, God rest them! Sure, you're a nice little gerrl, an' I give you great welcome and the hope you'll do well. Come along wit' me now. Your Aunty Biddy's jealous to put her two eyes on you, an' we never getting the news you'd come till late this morning. 'I'll go fetch Nora for you,' says I, to contint her. 'They'll be tarked out at Duffy's by this time,' says I."

"Oh, I'm full o' tark yet!" protested Nora gayly. "Coom on, then, Uncle Patsy!" and she gave him her strong young hand as he rose.

"An' how do you be likin' Ameriky?"

asked the pleased old man, as they walked along.

"I like Ameriky fine," answered the girl gravely. She was taller than he, though she looked so slender and so young. "I was very downhearted, too, l'avin' home and me mother, but I'll go back to it some day, God willing, sir; I couldn't die wit'out seeing me mother again. I'm all over the place here since daybreak. I think I'd like work best on the railway," and she turned toward him with a resolved and serious look.

"Wisha! there's no work at all for a girl like you on the Road," said Uncle Patsy patiently. "You've a bit to learn yet, sure; 't is the mill you mane."

"There'll be plinty work to do. I always thought at home, when I heard the folks tarking, that I'd get work on the railway when I'd come to Ameriky. Yis, indeed, sir!" continued Nora earnestly. "I was looking at the mills just now, and I heard the great n'ise from them. I'd never be afther shutting meself up in anny mill out of the good air. I've no call to go to jail yet in thim mill walls. Perhaps there'd be somebody working next me that I'd never get to like, sir."

There was something so convinced and decided about these arguments that Uncle Patsy, usually the calm autocrat of his young relatives, had nothing whatever to say. Nora was gently keeping step with his slow gait. She had won his heart once for all when she called him by the old boyish name her mother used forty years before, when they played together by the Wishing Brook.

"I wonder do you know a b'y named Johnny O'Callahan?" inquired Nora presently, in a somewhat confidential tone; "a pritty b'y that's working on the railway; I seen him last night and I coming here; he ain't a guard at all, but a young fellow that minds the brakes. We stopped a long while out there; somethin' got off the rails, and he adwised wit' me, seeing I was a stranger. He said he knew you, sir."

"Oh, yes, Johnny O'Callahan. I know him well; he's a nice b'y, too," answered Patrick Quin approvingly.

"Yis, sir, a pritty b'y," said Nora, and her color brightened for an instant, but she said no more.

## II.

Mike Duffy and his wife came into the Quins' kitchen one week-day night, dressed in their Sunday clothes; they had been making a visit to their well-married daughter in Lawrence. Patrick Quin's chair was comfortably tipped back against the wall, and Bridget, who looked somewhat gloomy, was putting away the white supper-dishes.

"Where's Nora?" demanded Mike Duffy, after the first salutations.

"You may well say it; I'm afther missing her every hour in the day," lamented Bridget Quin.

"Nora's gone into business on the Road then, so she has," said Patrick, with an air of fond pride. He was smoking, and in his shirt-sleeves; his coat lay on the wooden settee at the other side of the room.

"Hand me me old coat there before you sit down; I want me pocket," he commanded, and Mike obeyed. Mary Ann, fresh from her journey, began at once to give a spirited account of her daughter's best room and general equipment for housekeeping, but she suddenly became aware that the tale was of secondary interest.

When the narrator stopped for breath there was a polite murmur of admiration, but her husband boldly repeated his question. "Where's Nora?" he insisted, and the Quins looked at each other and laughed.

"Ourselves is old hins that's hatched ducks," confessed Patrick. "Ain't I afther telling you she's gone into trade on the Road?" and he took his pipe from his mouth, — that after-supper pipe which neither prosperity nor adversity was apt to interrupt. "She's set up for herself overright the long switch, down there at Birch Plains. Nora'll soon be rich, the cr'atur'; her mind was on it from the first start; 't was from one o' them O'Callahan b'ys she got the notion, the night she come here first a greenhorn."

"Well, well, she's lost no time; ain't she got the invintion!" chuckled Mr. Michael Duffy, who delighted in the activity of others. "What excuse had she for Birch Plains? There's no town to it."

"'T was a chance on the Road she mint to have from the first," explained the proud uncle, forgetting his pipe altogether; "'t was that she told me the first day she came out, an' she walking along going home wit' me to her dinner; 't was the first speech I had wit' Nora. ' 'T is the mills you mane?' says I. 'No, no, Uncle Patsy!' says she, 'it ain't the mills at all, at all; 't is on the Road I'm going.' I t'ought she'd some wild notion she'd soon be laughing at, but she settled down very quiet-like with Aunty Biddy here, knowing yourselves to be going to Lawrence, and I told her stay as long as she had a mind. Wisha, she'd an old apron on her in five minutes' time, an' took hold wit' the wash, and wint singing like a blackbird out in the yard at the line. 'Sit down, Aunty!' says she; 'you're not so light-stepping as me, an' I'll tell you all the news from home; an' I'll get the dinner, too, when I've done this,' says she. Wisha, but she's the good cook for such a young thing; 't is Bridget says it as well as meself. She made a stew that day; 't was like the ones her mother made Sundays, she said, if they'd be lucky in getting a piece of meat; 't was a fine-tasting stew, too; she thinks we're all rich over here. 'So we are, me dear!' says I, 'but every one don't have the sinse to believe it.'"

"Spake for yourselves!" exclaimed one of the listeners. "You do be like Father

Ross, always pr'achin' that we'd best want less than want more. He takes honest folks for fools, poor man," said Mary Ann Duffy, who had no patience at any time with new ideas.

"An' so she wint on the next two or t'ree days," said Patrick approvingly, without noticing the interruption, "being as quiet as you'd ask, and being said by her aunt in everything; and she wouldn't let on she was homesick, but she'd no tark of anything but the folks at Dunkinny. When there'd be nothing to do for an hour she'd slip out and be gone wit' herself for a little while, and be very still comin' in. Last Thursday, after supper, she ran out; but by the time I'd done me pipe, back she came flying in at the door.

"'I'm going off to a place called Birch Plains to-morrow morning, on the nine, Uncle Patsy,' says she; 'do you know where it is?' says she. 'I do,' says I; ''t was not far from it I broke me leg wit' the dam' derrick. 'T was to Jerry Ryan's house they took me first. There's no town there at all; 't is the only house in it; Ryan's the switchman.'

"'Would they take me to lodge for a

while, I d' know?' says she, havin' great
business. 'What'd ye be afther in a place
like that?' says I. 'Ryan's got girls himself, an' they're all here in the mills, goin'
home Saturday nights, 'less there's some
show or some dance. There's no money
out there.' She laughed then an' wint back
to the door, and in come Mickey Dunn
from McLoughlin's store, lugging the size
of himself of bundles. 'What's all this?'
says I; ''t ain't here they belong; I bought
nothing to-day.' 'Don't be scolding!' says
she, and Mickey got out of it laughing.
'I'm going to be cooking for meself in the
morning!' says she, with her head on one
side, like a cock-sparrow. 'You lind me
the price o' the fire and I'll pay you in
cakes,' says she, and off she wint then to
bed. 'T was before day I heard her at the
stove, and I smelt a baking that made me
want to go find it, and when I come out
in the kitchen she'd the table covered with
her cakeens, large and small. 'What's all
this whillalu, me topknot-hin?' says I. 'Ate
that,' says she, and hopped back to the oven-
door. Her aunt come out then, scolding
fine, and whin she saw the great baking she
dropped down in a chair like she'd faint

and her breath all gone. 'We 'ont ate them in ten days,' says she; 'no, not till the blue mould has struck them all, God help us!' says she. 'Don't bother me,' says Nora; 'I'm goin' off with them all on the nine. Uncle Patsy 'll help me wit' me basket.'

"'Uncle Patsy 'ont now,' says Bridget. Faix, I thought she was up with one o' them t'ree days' scolds she'd have when she was young and the childre' all the one size. You could hear the bawls of her a mile away.

"'Whishper, dear,' says Nora; 'I don't want to be livin' on anny of me folks, and Johnny O'Callahan said all the b'ys was wishing there was somebody would kape a clane little place out there at Birch Plains, — with something to ate and the like of a cup of tay. He says 'tis a good little chance; them big trains does all be waiting there tin minutes and fifteen minutes at a time, and everybody's hungry. "I'll thry me luck for a couple o' days," says I; "'tis no harm, an' I've tin shillings o' me own that Father Daley gave me wit' a grand blessing and I l'aving home behind me." ' "

"'What tark you have of Johnny O'Callahan,' says I.

"Look at this now!" continued the proud uncle, while Aunt Biddy sat triumphantly watching the astonished audience; "'t is a letter I got from the shild last Friday night," and he brought up a small piece of paper from his coat-pocket. "She writes a good hand, too. 'Dear Uncle Patsy,' says she, 'this leaves me well, thanks be to God. I'm doing the roaring trade with me cakes; all Ryan's little boys is selling on the trains. I took one pound three the first day: 't was a great excursion train got stuck fast and they'd a hot box on a wheel keeping them an hour and two more trains stopping for them; 't would be a very pleasant day in the old country that anybody'd take a pound and three shillings. Dear Uncle Patsy, I want a whole half-barrel of that same flour and ten pounds of sugar, and I'll pay it back on Sunday. I sind respects and duty to Aunty Bridget and all friends; this l'aves me in great haste. I wrote me dear mother last night and sint her me first pound, God bless her.'"

"Look at that for you now!" exclaimed

Mike Duffy. "Did n't I tell every one here she was fine an' smart?"

"She 'll be soon Prisident of the Road," announced Aunt Mary Ann, who, having been energetic herself, was pleased to recognize the same quality in others.

"She don't be so afraid of the worruk as the worruk's afraid of her," said Aunt Bridget admiringly. "She 'll have her fling for a while and be glad to go in and get a good chance in the mill, and be kaping her plants in the weave-room windows this winter with the rest of the girls. Come, tell us all about Elleneen and the baby. I ain't heard a word about Lawrence yet," she added politely.

"Ellen's doing fine, an' it 's a pritty baby. She 's got a good husband, too, that l'aves her her own way and the keep of his money every Saturday night," said Mary Ann; and the little company proceeded to the discussion of a new and hardly less interesting subject. But before they parted, they spoke again of Nora.

"She 's a fine, crabbed little gerrl, that little Nora," said Mr. Michael Duffy.

"Thank God, none o' me childre' is redheaded on me; they 're no more to be let an' held than a flick o' fire," said Aunt Mary Ann. "Who'd ever take the notion to be setting up business out there on the Birchy Plains?"

"Ryan's folks'll look after her, sure, the same as ourselves," insisted Uncle Patsy hopefully, as he lighted his pipe again. It was like a summer night; the kitchen windows were all open, the month of May was nearly at an end, and there was a sober croaking of frogs in the low fields that lay beyond the village.

## III.

"Where's Nora?" Young Johnny O'Callahan was asking the question; the express had stopped for water, and he seemed to be the only passenger; this was his day off.

Mrs. Ryan was sitting on her doorstep to rest in the early evening; her husband had been promoted from switch-tender to boss of the great water-tank which was just beginning to be used, and there was talk of further improvements and promotions at Birch Plains; but the good-natured wife sensibly declared that the better off a woman was, the harder she always had to work.

She took a long look at Johnny, who was dressed even more carefully than if it were a pleasant Sunday.

"This don't be your train, annyway," she answered, in a meditative tone. "How come you here now all so fine, I'd like to know, riding in the cars like a lord; ain't you brakeman yet on old twinty-four?"

"'Deed I am, Mrs. Ryan; you wouldn't be afther grudging a boy his day off? Where's Nora?"

"She's gone up the road a bitteen," said Mrs. Ryan, as if she suddenly turned to practical affairs. "She's worked hard the day, poor shild! and she took the cool of the evening, and the last bun she had left, and wint away with herself. I kep' the taypot on the stove for her, but she'd have none at all, at all!"

The young man turned away, and Mrs. Ryan looked after him with an indulgent smile. "He's a pritty b'y," she said. "I'd like well if he'd give a look at one o' me own gerrls; Julia, now, would look well walking with him, she's so dark. He's got money saved. I saw the first day he come after the cakeens 't was the one that baked them was in his mind. She's lucky, is Nora; well, I'm glad of it."

It was fast growing dark, and Johnny's eyes were still dazzled by the bright lights of the train as he stepped briskly along the narrow country road. The more he had seen Nora and the better he liked her, the less she would have to say to him, and tonight he meant to find her and have a talk. He had only succeeded in getting half a dozen words at a time since the night of their first meeting on the slow train, when she had gladly recognized the peculiar brogue of her own country-side, as Johnny called the names of the stations, and Johnny's quick eyes had seen the tired-looking, uncertain, yet cheerful little greenhorn in the corner of the car, and asked if she were not the niece that was coming out to Mrs. Duffy. He had watched the growth of her business with delight, and heard praises of the cakes and buns with willing ears; was it not his own suggestion that had laid the foundation of Nora's prosperity? Since their first meeting they had always greeted each other like old friends, but Nora grew more and more willing to talk with any of her breathless customers who hurried up the steep bank from the trains than with him. She would never take any pay for her wares from him, and for a week he had stopped coming himself and sent by a friend his money for the cakes; but one day poor Johnny's heart could not resist the temptation of going with the rest, and Nora had given him a happy look, straightforward and significant. There was no time for a word, but she picked out a crusty bun, and he took it and ran back without offering to pay. It was the best bun that a man ever ate. Nora was two months out now, and he had never walked with her an evening yet.

The shadows were thick under a long row of willows; there was a new moon, and a faint glow in the west still lit the sky. Johnny walked on the grassy roadside with his ears keen to hear the noise of a betraying pebble under Nora's light foot. Presently his heart beat loud and all out of time as a young voice began to sing a little way beyond.

Nora was walking slowly away, but Johnny stopped still to listen. She was singing "A Blacksmith Courted Me," one of the quaintest and sweetest of the old-country songs, as she strolled along in the soft-aired summer night. By the time she came to "My love's gone along the fields," Johnny hurried on to overtake her; he could hear the other verses some other time, — the bird was even sweeter than the voice.

Nora was startled for a moment, and stopped singing, as if she were truly a bird in a bush, but she did not flutter away. "Is it yourself, Mister Johnny?" she asked soberly, as if the frank affection of the song had not been assumed.

"It's meself," answered Johnny, with equal discretion. "I come out for a mout'ful of air; it's very hot inside in the town. Days off are well enough in winter, but in summer you get a fine air on the train. 'T was well we both took the same direction. How is the business? All the b'ys are saying they'd be lost without it; sure there ain't a stomach of them but wants its bun, and they cried the length of the Road that day the thunder spoiled the baking."

"Take this," said Nora, as if she spoke to a child; "there's a fine crust of sugar on the top. 'T is one I brought out for me little supper, but I'm so pleased wit' bein' rich that I've no need at all for 'ating. An' I'm as tired as I'm rich," she added, with a sigh; "'t is few can say the same in this lazy land."

"Sure, let's ate it together; 't is a big little cakeen," urged Johnny, breaking the bun and anxiously offering Nora the larger piece. "I can like the taste of anything better by halves, if I've got company. You ought to have a good supper of tay and a piece of steak and some potaties rather than this! Don't be giving yourself nothing but the saved cakes, an' you working so hard!"

"'T is plenty days I'd a poorer supper when I was at home," said Nora sadly; "me father dying so young, and all of us begging at me mother's skirts. It's all me thought how will I get rich and give me mother all the fine things that's in the world. I wish I'd come over sooner, but it broke my heart whinever I'd think of being out of sight of her face. She looks old now, me mother does."

Nora may have been touched by Johnny's affectionate interest in her supper; she forgot all her shyness and drew nearer to him as they walked along, and he drew a little closer to her.

"My mother is dead these two years," he

said simply. "It makes a man be very lonesome when his mother's dead. I board with my sister that's married; I'm not much there at all. I do be thinking I'd like a house of my own. I've plinty saved for it."

"I said in the first of coming out that I'd go home again when I had fifty pounds," said Nora hastily, and taking the other side of the narrow road. "I've got a piece of it already, and I've sent back more beside. I thought I'd be gone two years, but some days I think I won't be so long as that."

"Why don't you be afther getting your mother out? 'T is so warm in the winter in a good house, and no dampness like there does be at home; and her brother and her sister both being here." There was deep anxiety in Johnny's voice.

"Oh, I don't know indeed!" said Nora. "She's very wake-hearted, is me mother; she'd die coming away from the old place and going to sea. No, I'm going to work meself and go home; I'll have presents, too, for everybody along the road, and the children 'll be running and skrieghing afther me, and they'll all get sweeties from me.

'T is a very poor neighborhood where we live, but a lovely sight of the say. It ain't often annybody comes home to it, but 't will be a great day then, and the poor old folks 'll all be calling afther me: 'Where's Nora?' 'Show me Nora!' 'Nora, sure, what have you got for me?' I 'ont forget one of them aither, God helping me!" said Nora, in a passion of tenderness and pity. "And oh, Johnny, then afther that I 'll see me mother in the door!"

Johnny was so close at her side that she slipped her hand into his, and neither of them stopped to think about so sweet and natural a pleasure. "I 'd like well to help you, me darlin'," said Johnny.

"Sure, an' was n't it yourself gave me all me good fortune?" exclaimed Nora. "I 'd be hard-hearted an' I forgot that so soon and you a Kerry boy, and me mother often spaking of your mother's folks before ever I thought of coming out!"

"Sure and would n't you spake the good word to your mother about me sometime, dear?" pleaded Johnny, openly taking the part of lover. Nora's hand was still in his; they were walking slowly in the summer night. "I loved you the first word I heard out of your mouth, — 't was like a thrush from home singing to me there in the train. I said when I got home that night, I 'd think of no other girl till the day I died."

"Oh!" said Nora, frightened with the change of his voice. "Oh, Johnny, 't is too soon. We never walked out this way before; you 'll have to wait for me; perhaps you 'd soon be tired of poor Nora, and the likes of one that 's all for saving and going home! You 'll marry a prittier girl than me some day," she faltered, and let go his hand.

"Indeed, I won't, then," insisted Johnny O'Callahan stoutly.

"Will you let me go home to see me mother?" said Nora soberly. "I 'm afther being very homesick, 't is the truth for me. I 'd lose all me courage if it wa'n't for the hope of that."

"I will, indeed," said Johnny honestly.

Nora put out her hand again, of her own accord. "I 'll not say no, then," she whispered in the dark. "I can't work long unless I do be happy, and — well, leave me free till the month's end, and maybe then I 'll say yes. Stop, stop!" she let go Johnny's hand, and hurried along by herself in the road, Johnny, in a transport of happiness, walking very fast to keep up. She reached a knoll where he could see her slender shape against the dim western sky. "Wait till I tell you; *whisper!*" said Nora eagerly. "You know there were some of the managers of the road, the superintendents and all those big ones, came to Birch Plains yesterday?"

"I did be hearing something," said Johnny, wondering.

"There was a quiet-spoken, nice old gentleman came asking me at the door for something to eat, and I being there baking; 't is my time in the morning whin the early trains does be gone, and I 've a fine stretch till the expresses are beginnin' to screech, — the tin, and the tin-thirty-two, and the Flying Aigle. I was in a great hurry with word of an excursion coming in the afternoon and me stock very low; I 'd been baking since four o'clock. He 'd no coat on him, 't was very warm; and I thought 't was some tramp. Lucky for me I looked again and I said, 'What are you wanting, sir?' and then I saw he 'd a beautiful shirt on him, and was very quiet and pleasant.

"'I came away wit'out me breakfast,'

says he. 'Can you give me something without too much throuble?' says he. 'Do you have anny of those buns there that I hear the men talking about?'

"'There's buns there, sir,' says I, 'and I'll make you a cup of tay or a cup of coffee as quick as I can,' says I, being pleased at the b'ys giving me buns a good name to the likes of him. He was very hungry, too, poor man, an' I ran to Mrs. Ryan to see if she'd a piece of beefsteak, and my luck ran before me. He sat down in me little place and enjoyed himself well.

"'I had no such breakfast in tin years, me dear,' said he at the last, very quiet and thankful; and he l'aned back in the chair to rest him, and I cleared away, being in the great hurry, and he asking me how I come there, and I tolt him, and how long I'd been out, and I said it was two months and a piece, and she being always in me heart, I spoke of me mother, and all me great hopes.

"Then he sat and thought as if his mind wint to his own business, and I wint on wit' me baking. Says he to me after a while, 'We're going to build a branch road across country to connect with the great mountain-roads,' says he; 'the junction's going to be right here; 't will give you a big market for your buns. There'll be a lunch-counter in the new station; do you think you could run it?' says he, spaking very sober.

"'I'd do my best, sir, annyway,' says I. 'I'd look out for the best of help. Do you know Patrick Quin, sir, that was hurt on the Road and gets a pinsion, sir?'

"'I do,' says he. 'One of the best men that ever worked for this company,' says he.

"'He's me mother's own brother, then, an' he'll stand by me,' says I; and he asked me me name and wrote it down in a book he got out of the pocket of him. 'You shall have the place if you want it,' says he; 'I won't forget,' and off he wint as quiet as he came."

"Tell me who was it?" said Johnny O'Callahan, listening eagerly.

"Mr. Ryan come tumbling in the next minute, spattered with water from the tank. 'Well, then,' says he, 'is your fine company gone?'

"'He is,' says I. 'I don't know is it some superintendent? He's a nice man, Mr. Ryan, whoiver he is,' says I.

" ' 'T is the Gineral Manager of the Road,' says he; 'that's who he is, sure!'"

"My apron was all flour, and I was in a great rage wit' so much to do, but I did the best I could for him. I'd do the same for anny one so hungry," concluded Nora modestly.

"Ain't you got the Queen's luck!" exclaimed Johnny admiringly. "Your fortune's made, me dear. I'll have to come off the road to help you."

"Oh, two good trades 'll be better than one!" answered Nora gayly, "and the big station nor the branch road are n't building yet."

"What a fine little head you 've got," said Johnny, as they reached the house where the Ryans lived, and the train was whistling that he meant to take back to town. "Goodnight, annyway, Nora; nobody 'd know from the size of your head there could be so much inside in it!"

"I'm lucky, too," announced Nora serenely. "No, I won't give you me word till the ind of the month. You may be seeing another gerrl before that, and calling me the red-headed sparrow. No, I'll wait a good while, and see if the two of us can't do better. Come, run away, Johnny. I'll drop asleep in the road; I'm up since four o'clock making me cakes for plinty b'ys like you."

The Ryans were all abed and asleep, but there was a lamp burning in the kitchen. Nora blew it out as she stole into her hot little room. She had waited, talking eagerly with Johnny, until they saw the headlight of the express like a star, far down the long line of double track.

## IV.

The summer was not ended before all the railroad men knew about Johnny O'Callahan's wedding and all his good fortune. They boarded at the Ryans' at first, but late in the evenings Johnny and his wife were at work, building as if they were birds. First, there was a shed with a broad counter for the cakes, and a table or two, and the boys did not fail to notice that Nora had a good sisterly work-basket ready, and was quick to see that a useful button was off or a stitch needed. The next fortnight saw a room added to this, where Nora had her own stove, and cooking went on steadily. Then there was another room with white muslin curtains at the windows, and scarlet-runner beans made haste to twine themselves to a line of strings for shade. Johnny would unload a few feet of clean pine boards from the freight train, and within a day or two they seemed to be turned into a wing of the small castle by some easy magic. The boys used to lay wagers and keep watch, and there was a cheer out of the engine-cab and all along the platforms one day when a tidy sty first appeared and a neat pig poked his nose through the fence of it. The buns and biscuits grew famous; customers sent for them from the towns up and down the long railroad line, and the story of thrifty, kind-hearted little Nora and her steady young husband was known to a surprising number of persons. When the branch road was begun, Nora and Johnny took a few of their particular friends to board, and business was further increased. On Sunday they always went into town to mass and visited their uncles and aunts and Johnny's sister. Nora never said that she was tired, and almost never was cross. She counted her money every Saturday night, and took it to Uncle Patsy to put into the bank. She had long talks about her mother with Uncle Patsy, and he always wrote home for her when she had no time. Many a pound went across the sea in the letters, and so another summer came; and one morning when Johnny's train stopped, Nora stood at the door of the little house and held a baby in her arms for all the boys to see. She was white as a ghost and as happy as a queen. "I'll be making the buns again pretty soon," she cried cheerfully. "Have courage, boys; 't won't be long first; this one'll be selling them for me on the Flying Aigle, don't you forget it!" And there was a great ringing of the engine-bell a moment after, when the train started.

## V.

It was many and many a long month after this that an old man and a young woman and a baby were journeying in a side-car along one of the smooth Irish roads into County Kerry. They had left the railroad an hour before; they had landed early that morning at the Cove of Cork. The side-car was laden deep with bundles and boxes, but the old horse trotted briskly along until the gossoon who was driving turned into a cart-track that led through a furzy piece of wild pasture-ground up toward the dark rain-clouded hills.

"See, over there's Kinmare!" said the old man, looking back. "Manny's the day I've trudged it and home again. Oh, I know all this country; I knew it well whin ayther of you wa'n't born!"

"God be thanked, you did, sir!" responded the gossoon, with fervent admiration. He was a pleasant-looking lad in a ragged old coat and an absolutely roofless hat, through which his bright hair waved in the summer wind. "Och, but the folks'll be looking out of all the doors to see you come. I'll be afther saying I never drove anny party with so rich a heart; there ain't a poor soul that asked a pinny of us since we left Bantry but she's got the shillin'. Look a' the flock coming now, sir, out of that house. There's the four-legged lady that pays the rint watchin' afther them from the door, too. They think you're a gintleman that's shootin', I suppose. 'T is Tom Flaherty's house, poor crathur; he died last winter, God rest him; 't was very inconvanient for him an' every one at the time, wit' snow on the ground and a great dale of sickness and distress. Father Daley, poor man, had to go to the hospital in Dublin wit' himself to get a leg cut off, and we'd nothing but rain out of the sky afther that till all the stones in the road was floatin' to the top."

"Son of old John Flaherty, I suppose?" asked the traveler, with a knowing air, after he had given the eager children some pennies and gingerbread, out of a great package. One of the older girls knew Nora and climbed to the spare seat at her side to join the company. "Son of old John Flaherty, I suppose, that was there before? There was Flahertys there and I l'aving home more than thirty-five years ago."

"Sure there's plinty Flahertys in it now, glory be to God!" answered the charioteer, with enthusiasm. "I'd have no mother meself but for the Flahertys." He leaped down to lead the stumbling horse past a deep rut and some loose stones, and beckoned the little girl sternly from her proud seat. "Run home, now!" he said, as she obeyed: "I'll give you a fine drive an' I coming down the hill;" but she had joined the travelers with full intent, and trotted gayly alongside like a little dog.

The old passenger whispered to his companion that they'd best double the gossoon's money, or warm it with two or three shillings extra, at least, and Nora nodded her prompt approval. "The old folks are all getting away; we'd best give a bitteen to the young ones they've left afther them," said Uncle Patsy, by way of excuse. "Och, there's more beggars between here and Queenstown than you'd find in the whole of Ameriky."

It seemed to Nora as if her purseful of money were warm against her breast, like another heart; the sixpences in her pocket all felt warm to her fingers and hopped by themselves into the pleading hands that were stretched out all along the way. The sweet clamor of the Irish voices, the ready blessings, the frank requests to those returning from America with their fortunes made, were all delightful to her ears. How she had dreamed of this day, and how the sun and shadows were chasing each other over these upland fields at last! How close the blue sea looked to the dark hills! It seemed as if the return of one prosperous child gave joy to the whole landscape. It was the old country the same as ever, — old Mother Ireland in her green gown, and the warm heart of her ready and unforgetting. As for Nora, she could only leave a wake of silver sixpences behind her, and when these were done, a duller trail of ha'pennies; and the air was full of blessings as she passed along the road to Dunkenny.

By this time Nora had stopped talking and laughing. At first everybody on the road seemed like her near relation, but the last minutes seemed like hours, and now and then a tear went shining down her cheek. The old man's lips were moving, — he was saying a prayer without knowing it; they were almost within sight of home. The poor little white houses, with their high gable-ends and weather-beaten thatch, that stood about the fields among the green hedges; the light shower that suddenly fell out of the clear sky overhead, made an old man's heart tremble in his breast. Round the next slope of the hill they should see the old place.

The wheel-track stopped where you turned off to go to the Donahoe farm, but no old Mary was there to give friendly welcome. The old man got stiffly down from the side-car and limped past the gate with a sigh; but Nora hurried ahead, carrying the big baby, not because he could n't walk, but because he could. The young son had inherited his mother's active disposition, and would run straight away like a spider the minute his feet were set to the ground. Now and then, at the sight of a bird or a flower in the grass, he struggled to get down. "Whisht, now!" Nora would say; "and are n't you going to see Granny indeed? Keep aisy now, darlin'!"

The old heart and the young heart were beating alike as these exiles followed the narrow footpath round the shoulder of the great hill; they could hear the lambs bleat and the tinkling of the sheep-bells that sweet May morning. From the lower hillside came the sound of voices. The neighbors had seen them pass, and were calling to each other across the fields. Oh, it was home, home! the sight of it, and the smell of the salt air and the flowers in the bog, the look of the early white mushrooms in the sod, and the song of the larks overhead and the blackbirds in the hedges! Poor Ireland was gay-hearted in the spring weather, and Nora was there at last. "Oh, thank God, we 're safe home!" she said again. "Look, here 's the Wishing Brook; d' ye mind it?" she called back to the old man.

"I mind everything the day, no fear for me," said Patrick Quin.

The great hillside before them sloped up to meet the blue sky, the golden gorse spread its splendid tapestry against the green pasture. There was the tiny house, the one house in Ireland for Nora; its very windows watched her coming. A whiff of turf-smoke flickered above the chimney, the white walls were as white as the clouds above; there was a figure moving about inside the house, and a bent little woman in her white frilled cap and a small red shawl pinned about her shoulders came and stood in the door.

"Oh, me mother, me mother!" cried Nora; then she dropped the baby in the soft grass, and flew like a pigeon up the hill and into her mother's arms.

## VI.

The gossoon was equal to emergencies; he put down his heavier burden of goods and picked up the baby, lest it might run back to America. "God be praised, what's this coming afther ye?" exclaimed the mother, while Nora, weeping for joy, ran past her into the house. "Oh, God bless the shild that I thought I'd never see. Oh!" and she looked again at the stranger, the breathless old man with the thorn stick, whom everybody had left behind. " 'T is me brother Patsy! Oh, me heart's broke wit' joy!" and she fell on her knees among the daisies.

"It's meself, then!" said Mr. Patrick Quin. "How are ye the day, Mary? I always t'ought I'd see home again, but 't was Nora enticed me now. Johnny O'Callahan's a good son to ye; he'd liked well to come with us, but he gets short l'ave on the Road, and he has a fine, steady job; he'll see after the business, too, while we're gone; no, I couldn't let the two childer cross the say alone. Coom now, don't be sayin' anny more prayers; sure, we'll be sayin' them together in the old church coom Sunday.

"There, don't cry, Mary, don't cry, now! Coom in in the house! Sure, all the folks sint their remimbrance, and hoped you'd come back with us and stay a long while. That's our intintion, too, for you," continued Patrick, none the less tearful himself because he was so full of fine importance; but nobody could stop to listen after the first moment, and the brother and sister were both crying faster than they could talk. A minute later the spirit of the hostess rose to her great occasion.

"Go, chase those white hins," Nora's mother commanded the gossoon, who had started back to bring up more of the rich-looking bundles from the side-car. "Run them up-hill now, or they'll fly down to Kinmare. Go now, while I stir up me fire and make a cup o' tay. 'T is the laste I can do whin me folks is afther coming so far!"

"God save all here!" said Uncle Patsy devoutly, as he stepped into the house. There sat little Nora with the tired baby in her arms; to tell the truth, she was crying now for lack of Johnny. She looked pale, but her eyes were shining, and a ray of sunlight fell through the door and brightened her red hair. She looked quite beautiful and radiant as she sat there.

"Well, Nora, ye're here, ain't you?" said the old man.

"Only this morning," said the mother, "whin I opened me eyes I says to meself: 'Where's Nora?' says I; 'she do be so long wit'out writing home to me;' look at her now by me own fire! Wisha, but what's all this whillalu and stramach down by the brook? Oh, see now! the folks have got word; all the folks is here! Coom out to them, Nora; give me the shild; coom out, Patsy boy!"

"Where's Nora? Where's Nora?" they could hear the loud cry coming, as all the neighbors hurried up the hill.

# BOLD WORDS AT THE BRIDGE.

## I.

"'WELL, now,' says I, 'Mrs. Con'ly,' says I, 'how ever you may tark, 't is nobody's business and I wanting to plant a few pumpkins for me cow in among me cabbages. I 've got the right to plant whatever I may choose, if it 's the divil of a crop of t'istles in the middle of me ground.' 'No ma'am, you ain't,' says Biddy Con'ly; 'you ain't got anny right to plant t'istles that 's not for the public good,' says she; and I being so hasty wit' me timper, I shuk me fist in her face then, and herself shuk her fist at me. Just then Father Brady come by, as luck ardered, an' recomminded us would we keep the peace. He knew well I 'd had my provocation; 't was to herself he spoke first. You 'd think she owned the whole corporation. I wished I 'd t'rown her over into the wather, so I did, before he come by at all. 'T was on the bridge the two of us were. I was stepping home by meself very quiet in the afthernoon to put me tay-kittle on for supper, and herself overtook me, — ain't she the bold thing!

"'How are you the day, Mrs. Dunl'avy?' says she, so mincin' an' preenin', and I knew well she'd put her mind on having words wit' me from that minute. I'm one that likes to have peace in the neighborhood, if it wa'n't for the likes of her, that makes the top of me head lift and clat' wit' rage like a pot-lid!"

"What was the matter with the two of you?" asked a listener, with simple interest.

"Faix indeed, 't was herself had a thrifle of melons planted the other side of the fince," acknowledged Mrs. Dunleavy. "She said the pumpkins would be the ruin of them intirely. I says, and 't was thrue for me, that I'd me pumpkins planted the week before she'd dropped anny old melon seed into the ground, and the same bein' already dwining from so manny bugs. Oh, but she's blackhearted to give me the lie about it, and say those poor things was all up, and she'd thrown lime on 'em to keep away their inemies when she first see me come out betune me cabbage rows. How well she knew what I might be doing! Me cabbages grows far apart and I'd plinty of room, and if a pumpkin vine gets attention you can entice it wherever you pl'ase and it'll grow fine and long, while the poor cabbages ates and grows fat and round, and no harm to annybody, but she must pick a quarrel with a quiet 'oman in the face of every one.

"We were on the bridge, don't you see, and plinty was passing by with their grins, and loitering and stopping afther they were behind her back to hear what was going on betune us. Annybody does be liking to get the sound of loud talk an' they having nothing better to do. Biddy Con'ly, seeing she was well watched, got the airs of a pr'acher, and set down whatever she might happen to be carrying and tried would she get the better of me for the sake of their admiration. Oh, but wa'n't she all drabbled and wet from the roads, and the world knows meself for a very tidy walker!

"'Clane the mud from your shoes if you're going to dance;' 'twas all I said to her, and she being that mad she did be stepping up and down like an old turkey-hin, and shaking her fist all the time at me. 'Coom now, Biddy,' says I, 'what put you out so?' says I. 'Sure, it creeps me skin when I looks at you! Is the pig dead,' says I, ' or anny little thing happened to you, ma'am? Sure this is far beyond the rights of a few pumpkin seeds that has just cleared the ground!' and all the folks laughed. I'd no call to have tark with Biddy Con'ly before them idle b'ys and gerrls, nor to let the two of us become their laughing-stock. I tuk up me basket, being ashamed then, and I meant to go away, mad as I was. 'Coom, Mrs. Con'ly!' says I, 'let bygones be bygones; what's all this whillalu we're afther having about nothing?' says I very pleasant.

"'May the divil fly away with you, Mary Dunl'avy!' says she then, 'spoiling me garden ground, as every one can see, and full of your bold talk. I'll let me hens out into it this afternoon, so I will,' says she, and a good deal more. 'Hold off,' says I, 'and remember what fell to your aunt one day when she sint her hins in to pick a neighbor's piece, and while her own back was turned they all come home and had every sprouted bean and potatie heeled out in the hot sun, and all her fine lettuces picked into Irish lace. We've lived neighbors,' says I, 'thirteen years,' says I ; 'and we've often had words together above the fince,' says I, 'but we're neighbors yet, and we've no call to stand here in such spectacles and disgracing ourselves and each other. Coom, Biddy,' says I, again, going away with me basket and remimbering Father Brady's caution whin it was too late. Some o' the b'ys went off too, thinkin' 't was all done.

"'I don't want anny o' your Coom Biddy's,' says she, stepping at me, with a black stripe across her face, she was that destroyed with rage, and I stepped back and held up me basket between us, she being bigger than I, and I getting no chance, and herself slipped and fell, and her nose got a clout with the hard edge of the basket, it would trouble the saints to say how, and then I picked her up and wint home with her to thry and quinch the blood. Sure I was sorry for the crathur an' she having such a timper boiling in her heart.

"'Look at you now, Mrs. Con'ly,' says I, kind of soft, 'you 'ont be fit for mass these two Sundays with a black eye like this, and your face arl scratched, and every bliguard has gone the lingth of the town to tell tales of us. I'm a quiet 'oman,' says I, 'and I don't thank you,' says I, whin the blood was stopped, — 'no, I don't thank you for disgracin' an old neighbor like me. 'T is of our prayers and the grave we should be thinkin', and not be having bold words on the bridge.' Wisha! but I t'ought I was after spaking very quiet, and up she got and caught up the basket, and I dodged it by good luck, but after that I walked off and left her to satisfy her foolishness with b'ating the wall if it pl'ased her. I 'd no call for her company anny more, and I took a vow I 'd never spake a word to her again while the world stood. So all is over since then betune Biddy Con'ly and me. No, I don't look at her at all!"

## II.

Some time afterward, in late summer, Mrs. Dunleavy stood, large and noisy, but generous-hearted, addressing some remarks from her front doorway to a goat on the sidewalk. He was pulling some of her cherished foxgloves through the picket fence, and eagerly devouring their flowery stalks.

"How well you rache through an honest fince, you black pirate!" she shouted; but finding that harsh words had no effect, she took a convenient broom, and advanced to strike a gallant blow upon the creature's back. This had the simple effect of making him step a little to one side and modestly begin to nibble at a tuft of grass.

"Well, if I ain't plagued!" said Mrs. Dunleavy sorrowfully; "if I ain't throubled with every wild baste, and me cow that was some use gone dry very unexpected, and a neighbor that's worse than none at all. I've nobody to have an honest word with, and the morning being so fine and pleasant. Faix, I'd move away from it, if there was anny place I'd enjoy better. I've no heart except for me garden, me poor little crops is doing so well; thanks be to God, me cabbages is very fine. There does be those that overlooked me pumpkins for the poor cow; they're no size at all wit' so much rain."

The two small white houses stood close together, with their little gardens behind them. The road was just in front, and led down to a stone bridge which crossed the river to the busy manufacturing village beyond. The air was fresh and cool at that early hour, the wind had changed after a season of dry, hot weather; it was just the morning for a good bit of gossip with a neighbor, but summer was almost done, and the friends were not reconciled. Their respective acquaintances had grown tired of hearing the story of the quarrel, and the novelty of such a pleasing excitement had long been over. Mrs. Connelly was thumping away at a handful of belated ironing, and Mrs. Dunleavy, estranged and solitary, sighed as she listened to the iron. She was sociable by nature, and she had an impulse to go in and sit down as she used at the end of the ironing table.

"Wisha, the poor thing is mad at me yet, I know that from the sounds of her iron; 't was a shame for her to go picking a quarrel with the likes of me," and Mrs. Dunleavy sighed heavily and stepped down into her flower-plot to pull the distressed foxgloves back into their places inside the fence. The seed had been sent her from the old country, and this was the first year they had come into full bloom. She had been hoping that the sight of them would melt Mrs. Connelly's heart into some expression of friendliness, since they had come from adjoining parishes in old County Kerry. The goat lifted his head, and gazed at his enemy with mild interest; he was pasturing now by the roadside, and the foxgloves had proved bitter in his mouth.

Mrs. Dunleavy stood looking at him over the fence, glad of even a goat's company.

"Go 'long there; see that fine little tuft ahead now," she advised him, forgetful of his depredations. "Oh, to think I've nobody to spake to, the day!"

At that moment a woman came in sight round the turn of the road. She was a stranger, a fellow country-woman, and she carried a large newspaper bundle and a heavy handbag. Mrs. Dunleavy stepped out of the flower-bed toward the gate, and waited there until the stranger came up and stopped to ask a question.

"Ann Bogan don't live here, do she?"

"She don't," answered the mistress of the house, with dignity.

"I t'ought she didn't; you don't know where she lives, do you?"

"I don't," said Mrs. Dunleavy.

"I don't know ayther; niver mind, I'll find her; 'tis a fine day, ma'am."

Mrs. Dunleavy could hardly bear to let the stranger go away. She watched her far down the hill toward the bridge before she turned to go into the house. She seated herself by the side window next Mrs. Connelly's, and gave herself to her thoughts.

The sound of the flatiron had stopped when the traveler came to the gate, and it had not begun again. Mrs. Connelly had gone to her front door; the hem of her calico dress could be plainly seen, and the bulge of her apron, and she was watching the stranger quite out of sight. She even came out to the doorstep, and for the first time in many weeks looked with friendly intent toward her neighbor's house. Then she also came and sat down at her side window. Mrs. Dunleavy's heart began to leap with excitement.

"Bad cess to her foolishness, she does be afther wanting to come round; I'll not make it too aisy for her," said Mrs. Dunleavy, seizing a piece of sewing and forbearing to look up. "I don't know who Ann Bogan is, annyway; perhaps herself does, having lived in it five or six years longer than me. Perhaps she knew this woman by her looks, and the heart is out of her with wanting to know what she asked from me. She can sit there, then, and let her irons grow cold!

"There was Bogans living down by the brick mill when I first come here, neighbors to Flaherty's folks," continued Mrs. Dunleavy, more and more aggrieved. "Biddy Con'ly ought to know the Flahertys, they being her cousins. 'T was a fine loud-talking 'oman; sure Biddy might well enough have heard her inquiring of me, and have stepped out, and said if she knew Ann Bogan, and satisfied a poor stranger that was hunting the town over. No, I don't know anny one in the name of Ann Bogan, so I don't," said Mrs. Dunleavy aloud, "and there's nobody I can ask a civil question, with every one that ought to be me neighbors stopping their mouths, and keeping black grudges whin 't was meself got all the offince."

"Faix 't was meself got the whack on me nose," responded Mrs. Connelly quite unexpectedly. She was looking squarely at the window where Mrs. Dunleavy sat behind the screen of blue mosquito netting. They were both conscious that Mrs. Connelly made a definite overture of peace.

"That one was a very civil-spoken 'oman that passed by just now," announced Mrs. Dunleavy, handsomely waiving the subject of the quarrel and coming frankly to the subject of present interest. "Faix, 't is a poor day for Ann Bogans; she'll find that out before she gets far in the place."

"Ann Bogans was plinty here once, then, God rest them! There was two Ann Bogans, mother and daughter, lived down by Flaherty's when I first come here. They died in the one year, too; 't is most thirty years ago," said Bridget Connelly, in her most friendly tone.

"'I'll find her,' says the poor 'oman as if she'd only to look; indeed, she's got the boldness," reported Mary Dunleavy, peace being fully restored.

"'T was to Flaherty's she'd go first, and they all moved to La'rence twelve years ago, and all she'll get from anny one would be the address of the cimet'ry. There was plenty here knowing to Ann Bogan once. That 'oman is one I've seen long ago, but I can't name her yet. Did she say who she was?" asked the neighbor.

"She did n't; I'm sorry for the poor 'oman, too," continued Mrs. Dunleavy, in the same spirit of friendliness. "She'd the expectin' look of one who came hoping to make a nice visit and find friends, and herself lugging a fine bundle. She'd the looks as if she'd lately come out; very decent, but old-fashioned. Her bonnet was made at home annyways, did ye mind? I'll lay it was bought in Cork when it was new, or maybe 't was from a good shop in Bantry or Kinmare, or some o' those old places. If she 'd seemed satisfied to wait, I 'd made her the offer of a cup of tay, but off she wint with great courage."

"I don't know but I 'll slip on me bonnet in the afthernoon and go find her," said Biddy Connelly, with hospitable warmth. "I 've seen her before, perhaps 't was long whiles ago at home."

"Indeed I thought of it myself," said Mrs. Dunleavy, with approval. "We 'd best wait, perhaps, till she 'd be coming back; there 's no train now till three o'clock. She might stop here till the five, and we 'll find out all about her. She 'll have a very lonesome day, whoiver she is. Did you see that old goat 'ating the best of me fairy-fingers that all bloomed the day?" she asked eagerly, afraid that the conversation might come to an end at any moment; but Mrs. Connelly took no notice of so trivial a subject.

"Me melons is all getting ripe," she announced, with an air of satisfaction. "There 's a big one must be ate now while we can; it 's down in the cellar cooling itself, an' I'd like to be dropping it, getting down the stairs. 'T was afther picking it I was before breakfast, itself having begun to crack open. Himself was the b'y that loved a melon, an' I ain't got the heart to look at it alone. Coom over, will ye, Mary?"

"'Deed then an' I will," said Mrs. Dunleavy, whose face was close against the mosquito netting. "Them old pumpkin vines was no good anny way; did you see how one of them had the invintion, and wint away up on the fince entirely wit' its great flowers, an' there come a rain on 'em, and so they all blighted? I'd no call to grow such stramming great things in my piece annyway, 'ating up all the goodness from me beautiful cabbages."

### III.

That afternoon the reunited friends sat banqueting together and keeping an eye on the road. They had so much to talk over and found each other so agreeable that it was impossible to dwell with much regret upon the long estrangement. When the melon was only half finished the stranger of the morning, with her large unopened bundle and the heavy handbag, was seen making her way up the hill. She wore such a weary and disappointed look that she was accosted and invited in by both the women, and being proved by Mrs. Connelly to be an old acquaintance, she joined them at their feast.

"Yes, I was here seventeen years ago for the last time," she explained. "I was working in Lawrence, and I came over and spent a fortnight with Honora Flaherty; then I wint home that year to mind me old mother, and she lived to past ninety. I'd nothing to keep me then, and I was always homesick afther America, so back I come to it, but all me old frinds and neighbors is changed and gone. Faix, this is the first welcome I've got yet from anny one. 'T is a beautiful welcome, too, — I'll get me apron out of me bundle, by your l'ave, Mrs. Con'ly. You've a strong resemblance to Flaherty's folks, dear, being cousins. Well, 't is a fine thing to have good neighbors. You an' Mrs. Dunleavy is very pleasant here so close together."

"Well, we does be having a hasty word now and then, ma'am," confessed Mrs. Dunleavy, "but ourselves is good neighbors this manny years. Whin a quarrel's about nothing betune friends, it don't count for much, so it don't."

"Most quarrels is the same way," said the stranger, who did not like melons, but accepted a cup of hot tea. "Sure, it always takes two to make a quarrel, and but one to end it; that's what me mother always told me, that never gave anny one a cross word in her life."

"'T is a beautiful melon," repeated Mrs. Dunleavy for the seventh time. "Sure, I'll plant a few seed myself next year; me pumpkins is no good afther all me foolish pride wit' 'em. Maybe the land don't suit 'em, but glory be to God, me cabbages is the size of the house, an' you'll git the pick of the best, Mrs. Con'ly."

"What's melons betune friends, or cabbages ayther, that they should ever make any trouble?" answered Mrs. Connelly handsomely, and the great feud was forever ended.

But the stranger, innocent that she was the harbinger of peace, could hardly understand why Bridget Connelly insisted upon her staying all night and talking over old times, and why the two women put on their bonnets and walked, one on either hand, to see the town with her that evening. As they crossed the bridge they looked at each other shyly, and then began to laugh.

"Well, I missed it the most on Sundays going all alone to mass," confessed Mary Dunleavy. "I'm glad there's no one here seeing us go over, so I am."

"'T was ourselves had bold words at the bridge, once, that we've got the laugh about now," explained Mrs. Connelly politely to the stranger.

# MARTHA'S LADY.

## I.

ONE day, many years ago, the old Judge Pyne house wore an unwonted look of gayety and youthfulness. The high-fenced green garden was bright with June flowers. Under the elms in the large shady front yard you might see some chairs placed near together, as they often used to be when the family were all at home and life was going on gayly with eager talk and pleasure-making; when the elder judge, the grandfather, used to quote that great author, Dr. Johnson, and say to his girls, " Be brisk, be splendid, and be public."

One of the chairs had a crimson silk shawl thrown carelessly over its straight back, and a passer-by, who looked in through the latticed gate between the tall gate-posts with their white urns, might think that this piece of shining East Indian color was a huge red lily that had suddenly bloomed against the syringa bush. There were certain windows thrown wide open that were usually shut, and their curtains were blowing free in the light wind of a summer afternoon; it looked as if a large household had returned to the old house to fill the prim best rooms and find them full of cheer.

It was evident to every one in town that Miss Harriet Pyne, to use the village phrase, had company. She was the last of her family, and was by no means old; but being the last, and wonted to live with people much older than herself, she had formed all the habits of a serious elderly person. Ladies of her age, something past thirty, often wore discreet caps in those days, especially if they were married, but being single, Miss Harriet clung to youth in this respect, making the one concession of keeping her waving chestnut hair as smooth and stiffly arranged as possible. She had been the dutiful companion of her father and mother in their latest years, all her elder brothers and sisters having married and gone, or died and gone, out of the old house. Now that she was left alone it seemed quite the best thing frankly to accept the fact of age, and to turn more resolutely than ever to the companionship of duty and serious books. She was more serious and given to routine than her elders themselves, as sometimes happened when the daughters of New England gentlefolks were brought up wholly in the society of their elders. At thirty-five she had more reluctance than her mother to face an unforeseen occasion, certainly more than her grandmother, who had preserved some cheerful inheritance of gayety and worldliness from colonial times.

There was something about the look of the crimson silk shawl in the front yard to make one suspect that the sober customs of the best house in a quiet New England village were all being set at defiance, and once when the mistress of the house came to stand in her own doorway, she wore the pleased but somewhat apprehensive look of a guest. In these days New England life held the necessity of much dignity and discretion of behavior; there was the truest hospitality and good cheer in all occasional festivities, but it was sometimes a self-conscious hospitality, followed by an inexorable return to asceticism both of diet and of behavior. Miss Harriet Pyne belonged to the very dullest days of New England, those which perhaps held the most priggishness for the learned professions, the most limited interpretation of the word "evangelical," and the pettiest indifference to large things. The outbreak of a desire for larger religious freedom caused at first a most determined reaction toward formalism, especially in small and quiet villages like Ashford, intently busy with their own concerns. It was high time for a little leaven to begin its work, in this moment when the great impulses of the war for liberty had died away and those of the coming war for patriotism and a new freedom had hardly yet begun.

The dull interior, the changed life of the old house, whose former activities seemed to have fallen sound asleep, really typified these larger conditions, and a little leaven had made its easily recognized appearance in the shape of a light-hearted girl. She was Miss Harriet's young Boston cousin, Helena Vernon, who, half-amused and half-impatient at the unnecessary sober-mindedness of her hostess and of Ashford in general, had set herself to the difficult task of gayety. Cousin Harriet looked on at a succession of ingenious and, on the whole, innocent attempts at pleasure, as she might have looked on at the frolics of a kitten who easily substitutes a ball of yarn for the uncertainties of a bird or a wind-blown leaf, and who may at any moment ravel the fringe of a sacred curtain-tassel in preference to either.

Helena, with her mischievous appealing eyes, with her enchanting old songs and her guitar, seemed the more delightful and even reasonable because she was so kind to everybody, and because she was a beauty. She had the gift of most charming manners. There was all the unconscious lovely ease and grace that had come with the good breeding of her city home, where many pleasant people came and went; she had no fear, one had almost said no respect, of the individual, and she did not need to think of herself. Cousin Harriet turned cold with apprehension when she saw the minister coming in at the front gate, and wondered in agony if Martha were properly attired to go to the door, and would by any chance hear the knocker; it was Helena who, delighted to have anything happen, ran to the door to welcome the Reverend Mr. Crofton as if he were a congenial friend of her own age. She could behave with more or less propriety during the stately first visit, and even contrive to lighten it with modest mirth, and to extort the confession that the guest had a tenor voice, though sadly out of practice ; but when the minister departed a little flattered, and hoping that he had not expressed himself too strongly for a pastor upon the poems of Emerson, and feeling the unusual stir of gallantry in his proper heart, it was Helena who caught the honored hat of the late Judge Pyne from its last resting-place in the hall, and holding it securely in both hands, mimicked the minister's self-conscious entrance. She copied his pompous and anxious expression in the dim parlor in such delicious fashion that Miss Harriet, who could not always extinguish a ready spark of the original sin of humor, laughed aloud.

"My dear!" she exclaimed severely the next moment, "I am ashamed of your being so disrespectful!" and then laughed again, and took the affecting old hat and carried it back to its place.

"I would not have had any one else see you for the world," she said sorrowfully as she returned, feeling quite self-possessed again, to the parlor doorway; but Helena still sat in the minister's chair, with her small feet placed as his stiff boots had been, and a copy of his solemn expression before they came to speaking of Emerson and of the guitar. "I wish I had asked him if he would be so kind as to climb the cherry-tree," said Helena, unbending a little at the discovery that her cousin would consent to laugh no more. "There are all those ripe cherries on the top branches. I can climb as high as he, but I can't reach far enough from the last branch that will bear me. The minister is so long and thin" —

"I don't know what Mr. Crofton would have thought of you; he is a very serious young man," said cousin Harriet, still ashamed of her laughter. "Martha will get the cherries for you, or one of the men. I should not like to have Mr. Crofton think you were frivolous, a young lady of your opportunities" — but Helena had escaped through the hall and out at the garden door at the mention of Martha's name. Miss Harriet Pyne sighed anxiously, and then smiled, in spite of her deep convictions, as she shut the blinds and tried to make the house look solemn again.

The front door might be shut, but the garden door at the other end of the broad hall was wide open upon the large sunshiny garden, where the last of the red and white peonies and the golden lilies, and the first of the tall blue larkspurs lent their colors in generous fashion. The straight box borders were all in fresh and shining green of their new leaves, and there was a fragrance of the old garden's inmost life and soul blowing from the honeysuckle blossoms on a long trellis. It was now late in the afternoon, and the sun was low behind great apple-trees at the garden's end, which threw their shadows over the short turf of the bleaching-green. The cherry-trees stood at one side in full sunshine, and Miss Harriet, who presently came to the garden steps to watch like a hen at the water's edge, saw her cousin's pretty figure in its white dress of India muslin hurrying across the grass. She was accompanied by the tall, ungainly shape of Martha the new maid, who, dull and indifferent to every one else, showed a surprising willingness and allegiance to the young guest.

"Martha ought to be in the dining-room, already, slow as she is; it wants but half an hour of tea-time," said Miss Harriet, as she turned and went into the shaded house. It was Martha's duty to wait at table, and there had been many trying scenes and defeated efforts toward her education. Martha was certainly very clumsy, and she seemed the clumsier because she had replaced her aunt, a most skillful person, who had but lately married a thriving farm and its prosperous owner. It must be confessed that Miss Harriet was a most bewildering instructor, and that her pupil's brain was easily confused and prone to blunders. The coming of Helena had been somewhat dreaded by reason of this incompetent service, but the guest took no notice of frowns or futile gestures at the first tea-table, except to establish friendly relations with Martha on her own account by a reassuring smile. They were about the same age, and next morning, before cousin Harriet came down, Helena showed by a word and a quick touch the right way to do something that had gone wrong and been impossible to understand the night before. A moment later the anxious mistress came in without suspicion, but Martha's eyes were as affectionate as a dog's, and there was a new look of hopefulness on her face ; this dreaded guest was a friend after all, and not a foe come from proud Boston to confound her ignorance and patient efforts.

The two young creatures, mistress and maid, were hurrying across the bleaching-green.

"I can't reach the ripest cherries," explained Helena politely, "and I think that Miss Pyne ought to send some to the minister. He has just made us a call. Why Martha, you haven't been crying again!"

"Yes 'm," said Martha sadly. "Miss Pyne always loves to send something to the minister," she acknowledged with interest, as if she did not wish to be asked to explain these latest tears.

"We'll arrange some of the best cherries in a pretty dish. I'll show you how, and you shall carry them over to the parsonage after tea," said Helena cheerfully, and Martha accepted the embassy with pleasure. Life was beginning to hold moments of something like delight in the last few days.

"You'll spoil your pretty dress, Miss Helena," Martha gave shy warning, and Miss Helena stood back and held up her skirts with unusual care while the country girl, in her heavy blue checked gingham, began to climb the cherry-tree like a boy.

Down came the scarlet fruit like bright rain into the green grass.

"Break some nice twigs with the cherries and leaves together; oh, you 're a duck, Martha!" and Martha, flushed with delight, and looking far more like a thin and solemn blue heron, came rustling down to earth again, and gathered the spoils into her clean apron.

That night at tea, during her handmaiden's temporary absence, Miss Harriet announced, as if by way of apology, that she thought Martha was beginning to understand something about her work. "Her aunt was a treasure, she never had to be told anything twice; but Martha has been as clumsy as a calf," said the precise mistress of the house. "I have been afraid sometimes that I never could teach her anything. I was quite ashamed to have you come just now, and find me so unprepared to entertain a visitor."

"Oh, Martha will learn fast enough because she cares so much," said the visitor eagerly. "I think she is a dear good girl. I do hope that she will never go away. I think she does things better every day, cousin Harriet," added Helena pleadingly, with all her kind young heart. The china-closet door was open a little way, and Martha heard every word. From that moment, she not only knew what love was like, but she knew love's dear ambitions. To have come from a stony hill-farm and a bare small wooden house, was like a cave-dweller's coming to make a permanent home in an art museum, such had seemed the elaborateness and elegance of Miss Pyne's fashion of life; and Martha's simple brain was slow enough in its processes and recognitions. But with this sympathetic ally and defender, this exquisite Miss Helena who believed in her, all difficulties appeared to vanish.

Later that evening, no longer homesick or hopeless, Martha returned from her polite errand to the minister, and stood with a sort of triumph before the two ladies, who were sitting in the front doorway, as if they were waiting for visitors, Helena still in her white muslin and red ribbons, and Miss Harriet in a thin black silk. Being happily self-forgetful in the greatness of the moment, Martha's manners were perfect, and she looked for once almost pretty and quite as young as she was.

"The minister came to the door himself, and returned his thanks. He said that cherries were always his favorite fruit, and he was much obliged to both Miss Pyne and Miss Vernon. He kept me waiting a few minutes, while he got this book ready to send to you, Miss Helena."

"What are you saying, Martha? I have sent him nothing!" exclaimed Miss Pyne, much astonished. "What does she mean, Helena?"

"Only a few cherries," explained Helena. "I thought Mr. Crofton would like them after his afternoon of parish calls. Martha and I arranged them before tea, and I sent them with our compliments."

"Oh, I am very glad you did," said Miss Harriet, wondering, but much relieved. "I was afraid" —

"No, it was none of my mischief," answered Helena daringly. "I did not think that Martha would be ready to go so soon. I should have shown you how pretty they looked among their green leaves. We put them in one of your best white dishes with the openwork edge. Martha shall show you to-morrow; mamma always likes to have them so." Helena's fingers were busy with the hard knot of a parcel.

"See this, cousin Harriet!" she announced proudly, as Martha disappeared round the corner of the house, beaming with the pleasures of adventure and success. "Look! the minister has sent me a book: Sermons on *what?* Sermons — it is so dark that I can't quite see."

"It must be his 'Sermons on the Seriousness of Life;' they are the only ones he has printed, I believe," said Miss Harriet, with much pleasure. "They are considered very fine discourses. He pays you a great compliment, my dear. I feared that he noticed your girlish levity."

"I behaved beautifully while he stayed," insisted Helena. "Ministers are only men," but she blushed with pleasure. It was certainly something to receive a book from its author, and such a tribute made her of more value to the whole reverent household. The minister was not only a man, but a bachelor, and Helena was at the age that best loves conquest; it was at any rate comfortable to be reinstated in cousin Harriet's good graces.

"Do ask the kind gentleman to tea! He needs a little cheering up," begged the siren in India muslin, as she laid the shiny black volume of sermons on the stone doorstep with an air of approval, but as if they had quite finished their mission.

"Perhaps I shall, if Martha improves as much as she has within the last day or two," Miss Harriet promised hopefully. "It is something I always dread a little when I am all alone, but I think Mr. Crofton likes to come. He converses so elegantly."

## II.

These were the days of long visits, before affectionate friends thought it quite worth while to take a hundred miles' journey merely to dine or to pass a night in one another's houses. Helena lingered through the pleasant weeks of early summer, and departed unwillingly at last to join her family at the White Hills, where they had gone, like other households of high social station, to pass the month of August out of town. The happy-hearted young guest left many lamenting friends behind her, and promised each that she would come back again next year. She left the minister a rejected lover, as well as the preceptor of the academy, but with their pride unwounded, and it may have been with wider outlooks upon the world and a less narrow sympathy both for their own work in life and for their neighbors' work and hindrances. Even Miss Harriet Pyne herself had lost some of the unnecessary provincialism and prejudice which had begun to harden a naturally good and open mind and affectionate heart. She was conscious of feeling younger and more free, and not so lonely. Nobody had ever been so gay, so fascinating, or so kind as Helena, so full of social resource, so simple and undemanding in her friendliness. The light of her young life cast no shadow on either young or old companions, her pretty clothes never seemed to make other girls look dull or out of fashion. When she went away up the street in Miss Harriet's carriage to take the slow train toward Boston and the gayeties of the new Profile House, where her mother waited impatiently with a group of Southern friends, it seemed as if there would never be any more picnics or parties in Ashford, and as if society had nothing left to do but to grow old and get ready for winter.

Martha came into Miss Helena's bedroom that last morning, and it was easy to see that she had been crying; she looked just as she did in that first sad week of homesickness and despair. All for love's sake she had been learning to do many things, and to do them exactly right; her eyes had grown quick to see the smallest chance for personal service. Nobody could be more humble and devoted; she looked years older than Helena, and wore already a touching air of caretaking.

"You spoil me, you dear Martha!" said Helena from the bed. "I don't know what they will say at home, I am so spoiled."

Martha went on opening the blinds to let in the brightness of the summer morning, but she did not speak.

"You are getting on splendidly, are n't you?" continued the little mistress. "You have tried so hard that you make me ashamed of myself. At first you crammed all the flowers together, and now you make them look beautiful. Last night cousin Harriet was so pleased when the table was so charming, and I told her that you did everything yourself, every bit. Won't you keep the flowers fresh and pretty in the house until I come back? It's so much pleasanter for Miss Pyne, and you'll feed my little sparrows, won't you? They're growing so tame."

"Oh, yes, Miss Helena!" and Martha looked almost angry for a moment, then she burst into tears and covered her face with her apron. "I could n't understand a single thing when I first came. I never had been anywhere to see anything, and Miss Pyne frightened me when she talked. It was you made me think I could ever learn. I wanted to keep the place, 'count of mother and the little boys; we 're dreadful hard pushed. Hepsy has been good in the kitchen; she said she ought to have patience with me, for she was awkward herself when she first came."

Helena laughed; she looked so pretty under the tasseled white curtains.

"I dare say Hepsy tells the truth," she said. "I wish you had told me about your mother. When I come again, some day we 'll drive up country, as you call it, to see her. Martha! I wish you would think of me sometimes after I go away. Won't you promise?" and the bright young face suddenly grew grave. "I have hard times myself; I don't always learn things that I ought to learn, I don't always put things straight. I wish you would n't forget me ever, and would just believe in me. I think it does help more than anything."

"I won't forget," said Martha slowly. "I shall think of you every day." She spoke almost with indifference, as if she had been asked to dust a room, but she turned aside quickly and pulled the little mat under the hot water jug quite out of its former straightness; then she hastened away down the long white entry, weeping as she went.

## III.

To lose out of sight the friend whom one has loved and lived to please is to lose joy out of life. But if love is true, there comes presently a higher joy of pleasing the ideal, that is to say, the perfect friend. The same old happiness is lifted to a higher level. As for Martha, the girl who stayed behind in Ashford, nobody's life could seem duller to those who could not understand; she was slow of step, and her eyes were almost always downcast as if intent upon incessant toil; but they startled you when she looked up, with their shining light. She was capable of the happiness of holding fast to a great sentiment, the ineffable satisfaction of trying to please one whom she truly loved. She never thought of trying to make other people pleased with herself; all she lived for was to do the best she could for others, and to conform to an ideal, which grew at last to be like a saint's vision, a heavenly figure painted upon the sky.

On Sunday afternoons in summer, Martha sat by the window of her chamber, a low-storied little room, which looked into the side yard and the great branches of an elm-tree. She never sat in the old wooden rocking-chair except on Sundays like this; it belonged to the day of rest and to happy meditation. She wore her plain black dress and a clean white apron, and held in her lap a little wooden box, with a brass ring on top for a handle. She was past sixty years of age and looked even older, but there was the same look on her face that it had sometimes worn in girlhood. She was the same Martha; her hands were old-looking and work-worn, but her face still shone. It seemed like yesterday that Helena Vernon had gone away, and it was more than forty years.

War and peace had brought their changes and great anxieties, the face of the earth was furrowed by floods and fire, the faces of mistress and maid were furrowed by smiles and tears, and in the sky the stars shone on as if nothing had happened. The village of Ashford added a few pages to its unexciting history, the minister preached, the people listened; now and then a funeral crept along the street, and now and then the bright face of a little child rose above the horizon of a family pew. Miss Harriet Pyne lived on in the large white house, which gained more and more distinction because it suffered no changes, save successive repaintings and a new railing about its stately roof. Miss Harriet herself had moved far beyond the uncertainties of an anxious youth. She had long ago made all her decisions, and settled all necessary questions; her scheme of life was as faultless as the miniature landscape of a Japanese garden, and as easily kept in order. The only important change she would ever be capable of making was the final change to another and a better world; and for that nature itself would gently provide, and her own innocent life.

Hardly any great social event had ruffled the easy current of life since Helena Vernon's marriage. To this Miss Pyne had gone, stately in appearance and carrying gifts of some old family silver which bore the Vernon crest, but not without some protest in her heart against the uncertainties of married life. Helena was so equal to a happy independence and even to the assistance of other lives grown strangely dependent upon her quick sympathies and instinctive decisions, that it was hard to let her sink her personality in the affairs of another. Yet a brilliant English match was not without its attractions to an old-fashioned gentlewoman like Miss Pyne, and Helena herself was amazingly happy; one day there had come a letter to Ashford, in which her very heart seemed to beat with love and self-forgetfulness, to tell cousin Harriet of such new happiness and high hope. "Tell Martha all that I say about my dear Jack," wrote the eager girl; "please show my letter to Martha, and tell her that I shall come home next summer and bring the handsomest and best man in the world to Ashford. I have told him all about the dear house and the dear garden; there never was such a lad to reach for cherries with his six-foot-two." Miss Pyne, wondering a little, gave the letter to Martha, who took it deliberately and as if she wondered too, and went away to read it slowly by herself. Martha cried over it, and felt a strange sense of loss and pain; it hurt her heart a little to read about the cherry-picking. Her idol seemed to be less her own since she had become the idol of a stranger. She never had taken such a letter in her hands before, but love at last prevailed, since Miss Helena was happy, and she kissed the last page where her name was written, feeling overbold, and laid the envelope on Miss Pyne's secretary without a word.

The most generous love cannot but long for reassurance, and Martha had the joy of being remembered. She was not forgotten when the day of the wedding drew near, but she never knew that Miss Helena had asked if cousin Harriet would not bring Martha to town; she should like to have Martha there to see her married. "She would help about the flowers," wrote the happy girl; "I know she will like to come, and I'll ask mamma to plan to have some one take her all about Boston and make her have a pleasant time after the hurry of the great day is over."

Cousin Harriet thought it was very kind

and exactly like Helena, but Martha would
be out of her element; it was most imprudent and girlish to have thought of such
a thing. Helena's mother would be far
from wishing for any unnecessary guest just
then, in the busiest part of her household,
and it was best not to speak of the invitation. Some day Martha should go to Boston if she did well, but not now. Helena
did not forget to ask if Martha had come,
and was astonished by the indifference of
the answer. It was the first thing which
reminded her that she was not a fairy
princess having everything her own way in
that last day before the wedding. She
knew that Martha would have loved to be
near, for she could not help understanding
in that moment of her own happiness the
love that was hidden in another heart.
Next day this happy young princess, the
bride, cut a piece of a great cake and put
it into a pretty box that had held one of her
wedding presents. With eager voices calling her, and all her friends about her, and
her mother's face growing more and more
wistful at the thought of parting, she still
lingered and ran to take one or two trifles
from her dressing-table, a little mirror and

some tiny scissors that Martha would remember, and one of the pretty handkerchiefs marked with her maiden name. These she put in the box too; it was half a girlish freak and fancy, but she could not help trying to share her happiness, and Martha's life was so plain and dull. She whispered a message, and put the little package into cousin Harriet's hand for Martha as she said good-by. She was very fond of cousin Harriet. She smiled with a gleam of her old fun; Martha's puzzled look and tall awkward figure seemed to stand suddenly before her eyes, as she promised to come again to Ashford. Impatient voices called to Helena, her lover was at the door, and she hurried away, leaving her old home and her girlhood gladly. If she had only known it, as she kissed cousin Harriet goodby, they were never going to see each other again until they were old women. The first step that she took out of her father's house that day, married, and full of hope and joy, was a step that led her away from the green elms of Boston Common and away from her own country and those she loved best, to a brilliant, much-varied foreign life, and to nearly all the sorrows and nearly all the joys that the heart of one woman could hold or know.

On Sunday afternoons Martha used to sit by the window in Ashford and hold the wooden box which a favorite young brother, who afterward died at sea, had made for her, and she used to take out of it the pretty little box with a gilded cover that had held the piece of wedding-cake, and the small scissors, and the blurred bit of a mirror in its silver case; as for the handkerchief with the narrow lace edge, once in two or three years she sprinkled it as if it were a flower, and spread it out in the sun on the old bleaching-green, and sat near by in the shrubbery to watch lest some bold robin or cherry-bird should seize it and fly away.

## IV.

Miss Harriet Pyne was often congratulated upon the good fortune of having such a helper and friend as Martha. As time went on this tall, gaunt woman, always thin, always slow, gained a dignity of behavior and simple affectionateness of look which suited the charm and dignity of the ancient house. She was unconsciously beautiful like a saint, like the picturesqueness of a lonely tree which lives to shelter unnumbered lives and to stand quietly in its place. There was such rustic homeliness and constancy belonging to her, such beautiful powers of apprehension, such reticence, such gentleness for those who were troubled or sick; all these gifts and graces Martha hid in her heart. She never joined the church because she thought she was not good enough, but life was such a passion and happiness of service that it was impossible not to be devout, and she was always in her humble place on Sundays, in the back pew next the door. She had been educated by a remembrance; Helena's young eyes forever looked at her reassuringly from a gay girlish face. Helena's sweet patience in teaching her own awkwardness could never be forgotten.

"I owe everything to Miss Helena," said Martha, half aloud, as she sat alone by the window; she had said it to herself a thousand times. When she looked in the little keepsake mirror she always hoped to see some faint reflection of Helena Vernon, but there was only her own brown old New England face to look back at her wonderingly.

Miss Pyne went less and less often to pay visits to her friends in Boston; there were very few friends left to come to Ashford and make long visits in the summer, and life grew more and more monotonous. Now and then there came news from across the sea and messages of remembrance, letters that were closely written on thin sheets of paper, and that spoke of lords and ladies, of great journeys, of the death of little children and the proud successes of boys at school, of the wedding of Helena Dysart's only daughter; but even that had happened years ago. These things seemed far away and vague, as if they belonged to a story and not to life itself; the true links with the past were quite different. There was the unvarying flock of ground-sparrows that Helena had begun to feed; every morning Martha scattered crumbs for them from the side doorsteps while Miss Pyne watched from the dining-room window, and they were counted and cherished year by year.

Miss Pyne herself had many fixed habits, but little ideality or imagination, and so at last it was Martha who took thought for her mistress, and gave freedom to her own good taste. After a while, without any one's observing the change, the every-day ways of doing things in the house came to be the stately ways that had once belonged only to the entertainment of guests. Happily both mistress and maid seized all possible chances for hospitality, yet Miss Harriet nearly always sat alone at her exquisitely served table with its fresh flowers, and the beautiful old china which Martha handled so lovingly that there was no good excuse for keeping it hidden on closet shelves. Every year when the old cherry-trees were in fruit, Martha carried the round white old English dish with a fretwork edge, full of pointed green leaves and scarlet cherries, to the minister, and his wife never quite understood why every year he blushed and looked so conscious of the pleasure, and thanked Martha as if he had received a very particular attention. There was no pretty suggestion toward the pursuit of the fine art of housekeeping in Martha's limited acquaintance with newspapers that she did not adopt; there was no refined old custom of the Pyne housekeeping that she consented to let go. And every day, as she had promised, she thought of Miss Helena, — oh, many times in every day: whether this thing would please her, or that be likely to fall in with her fancy or ideas of fitness. As far as was possible the rare news that reached Ashford through an occasional letter or the talk of guests was made part of Martha's own life, the history of her own heart. A worn old geography often stood open at the map of Europe on the lightstand in her room, and a little old-fashioned gilt button, set with a bit of glass like a ruby, that had broken and fallen from the trimming of one of Helena's dresses, was used to mark the city of her dwelling-place. In the changes of a diplomatic life Martha followed her lady all about the map. Sometimes the button was at Paris, and sometimes at Madrid; once, to her great anxiety, it remained long at St. Petersburg. For such a slow scholar Martha was not unlearned at last, since everything about life in these foreign towns was of interest to her faithful heart. She satisfied her own mind as she threw crumbs to the tame sparrows; it was all part of the same thing and for the same affectionate reasons.

## V.

One Sunday afternoon in early summer Miss Harriet Pyne came hurrying along the entry that led to Martha's room and called two or three times before its inhabitant could reach the door. Miss Harriet looked unusually cheerful and excited, and she held something in her hand. "Where are you, Martha?" she called again. "Come quick, I have something to tell you!"

"Here I am, Miss Pyne," said Martha, who had only stopped to put her precious box in the drawer, and to shut the geography.

"Who do you think is coming this very night at half-past six? We must have everything as nice as we can; I must see Hannah at once. Do you remember my cousin Helena who has lived abroad so long? Miss Helena Vernon, — the Honorable Mrs. Dysart, she is now."

"Yes, I remember her," answered Martha, turning a little pale.

"I knew that she was in this country, and I had written to ask her to come for a long visit," continued Miss Harriet, who did not often explain things, even to Martha, though she was always conscientious about the kind messages that were sent back by grateful guests. "She telegraphs that she means to anticipate her visit by a few days and come to me at once. The heat is beginning in town, I suppose. I daresay, having been a foreigner so long, she does not mind traveling on Sunday. Do you think Hannah will be prepared? We must have tea a little later."

"Yes, Miss Harriet," said Martha. She wondered that she could speak as usual, there was such a ringing in her ears. "I shall have time to pick some fresh strawberries; Miss Helena is so fond of our strawberries."

"Why, I had forgotten," said Miss Pyne, a little puzzled by something quite unusual in Martha's face. "We must expect to find Mrs. Dysart a good deal changed, Martha; it is a great many years since she was here; I have not seen her since her wedding, and she has had a great deal of trouble, poor girl. You had better open the parlor chamber, and make it ready before you go down."

"It is all ready," said Martha. "I can carry some of those little sweet-brier roses upstairs before she comes."

"Yes, you are always thoughtful," said Miss Pyne, with unwonted feeling.

Martha did not answer. She glanced at the telegram wistfully. She had never really suspected before that Miss Pyne knew nothing of the love that had been in her heart all these years; it was half a pain and half a golden joy to keep such a secret; she could hardly bear this moment of surprise.

Presently the news gave wings to her willing feet. When Hannah, the cook, who never had known Miss Helena, went to the parlor an hour later on some errand to her old mistress, she discovered that this stranger guest must be a very important person. She had never seen the tea-table look exactly as it did that night, and in the parlor itself there were fresh blossoming boughs in the old East India jars, and lilies in the paneled hall, and flowers everywhere, as if there were some high festivity.

Miss Pyne sat by the window watching, in her best dress, looking stately and calm; she seldom went out now, and it was almost time for the carriage. Martha was just coming in from the garden with the strawberries, and with more flowers in her apron. It was a bright cool evening in June, the golden robins sang in the elms, and the sun was going down behind the apple-trees at the foot of the garden. The beautiful old house stood wide open to the long-expected guest.

"I think that I shall go down to the gate," said Miss Pyne, looking at Martha for approval, and Martha nodded and they went together slowly down the broad front walk.

There was a sound of horses and wheels on the roadside turf: Martha could not see at first; she stood back inside the gate behind the white lilac-bushes as the carriage came. Miss Pyne was there; she was holding out both arms and taking a tired, bent little figure in black to her heart. "Oh, my Miss Helena is an old woman like me!" and Martha gave a pitiful sob; she had never dreamed it would be like this; this was the one thing she could not bear.

"Where are you, Martha?" called Miss Pyne. "Martha will bring these in; you have not forgotten my good Martha, Helena?" Then Mrs. Dysart looked up and smiled just as she used to smile in the old days. The young eyes were there still in the changed face, and Miss Helena had come.

That night Martha waited in her lady's room just as she used, humble and silent, and went through with the old unforgotten loving services. The long years seemed like days. At last she lingered a moment trying to think of something else that might be done, then she was going silently away, but Helena called her back. She suddenly knew the whole story and could hardly speak.

"Oh, my dear Martha!" she cried, "won't you kiss me good-night? Oh, Martha, have you remembered like this, all these long years!"

# THE COON DOG.

## I.

IN the early dusk of a warm September evening the bats were flitting to and fro, as if it were still summer, under the great elm that overshadowed Isaac Brown's house, on the Dipford road. Isaac Brown himself, and his old friend and neighbor John York, were leaning against the fence.

"Frost keeps off late, don't it?" said John York. "I laughed when I first heard about the circus comin'; I thought 't was so unusual late in the season. Turned out well, however. Everybody I noticed was returnin' with a palm-leaf fan. Guess they found 'em useful under the tent; 't was a master hot day. I saw old lady Price with her hands full o' those free advertisin' fans, as if she was layin' in a stock against next summer. Well, I expect she 'll live to enjoy 'em."

"I was right here where I 'm standin' now, and I see her as she was goin' by this mornin'," said Isaac Brown, laughing, and settling himself comfortably against the fence as if they had chanced upon a welcome subject of conversation. "I hailed her, same 's I gener'lly do. 'Where are you bound to-day, ma'am?' says I.

"'I 'm goin' over as fur as Dipford Centre,' says she. 'I 'm goin' to see my poor dear 'Liza Jane. I want to 'suage her grief; her husband, Mr. 'Bijah Topliff, has passed away.'

"'So much the better,' says I.

"'No; I never l'arnt about it till yisterday,' says she; an' she looked up at me real kind of pleasant, and begun to laugh.

"'I hear he 's left property,' says she, tryin' to pull her face down solemn. I give her the fifty cents she wanted to borrow to make up her car-fare and other expenses, an' she stepped off like a girl down tow'ds the depot.

"This afternoon, as you know, I 'd promised the boys that I 'd take 'em over to see the menagerie, and nothin' would n't do none of us any good but we must see the circus too; an' when we 'd just got posted on one o' the best high seats, mother she nudged me, and I looked right down front two, three rows, an' if there wa'n't Mis' Price, spectacles an' all, with her head right up in the air, havin' the best time you ever see. I laughed right out. She had n't taken no time to see 'Liza Jane; she wa'n't 'suagin' no grief for nobody till she 'd seen the circus. 'There,' says I, 'I do like to have anybody keep their young feelin's!'"

"Mis' Price come over to see our folks before breakfast," said John York. "Wife said she was inquirin' about the circus, but she wanted to know first if they could n't oblige her with a few trinkets o' mournin', seein' as how she 'd got to pay a mournin' visit. Wife thought 't was a bosom-pin, or somethin' like that, but turned out she wanted the skirt of a dress; 'most anything would do, she said."

"I thought she looked extra well startin' off," said Isaac, with an indulgent smile. "The Lord provides very handsome for such, I do declare! She ain't had no visible means o' support these ten or fifteen years back, but she don't freeze up in winter no more than we do."

"Nor dry up in summer," interrupted his friend; "I never did see such an able hand to talk."

"She's good company, and she's obliging an' useful when the women folks have their extra work progressin'," continued Isaac Brown kindly. "'T ain't much for a well-off neighborhood like this to support that old chirpin' cricket. My mother used to say she kind of helped the work along by 'livenin' of it. Here she comes now; must have taken the last train, after she had supper with 'Lizy Jane. You stay still; we're goin' to hear all about it."

The small, thin figure of Mrs. Price had to be hailed twice before she could be stopped.

"I wish you a good evenin', neighbors," she said. "I have been to the house of mournin'."

"Find 'Liza Jane in, after the circus?" asked Isaac Brown, with equal seriousness. "Excellent show, was n't it, for so late in the season?"

"Oh, beautiful; it was beautiful, I declare," answered the pleased spectator readily. "Why, I did n't see you, nor Mis' Brown. Yes; I felt it best to refresh my mind an' wear a cheerful countenance. When I see 'Liza Jane I was able to divert her mind consid'able. She was glad I went. I told her I'd made an effort, knowin' 't was so she had to lose the a'ternoon. 'Bijah left property, if he did die away from home on a foreign shore."

"You don't mean that 'Bijah Topliff's left anything!" exclaimed John York with interest, while Isaac Brown put both hands deep into his pockets, and leaned back in a still more satisfactory position against the gatepost.

"He enjoyed poor health," answered Mrs. Price, after a moment of deliberation, as if she must take time to think. "'Bijah never was one that scattereth, nor yet increaseth. 'Liza Jane's got some memories o' the past that's a good deal better than others; but he died somewheres out in Connecticut, or so she heard, and he's left a very val'able coon dog, — one he set a great deal by. 'Liza Jane said, last time he was to home, he priced that dog at fifty dollars. 'There, now, 'Liza Jane,' says I, right to her, when she told me, 'if I could git fifty dollars for that dog, I certain' would. Perhaps some o' the circus folks would like to buy him; they've taken in a stream o' money this day.' But 'Liza Jane ain't never inclined to listen to advice. 'T is a dreadful poor-spirited-lookin' creatur'. I don't want no right o' dower in him, myself."

"A good coon dog's worth somethin', certain," said John York handsomely.

"If he *is* a good coon dog," added Isaac Brown. "I wouldn't have parted with old Rover, here, for a good deal of money when he was right in his best days; but a dog like him's like one of the family. Stop an' have some supper, won't ye, Mis' Price?" — as the thin old creature was flitting off again. At that same moment this kind invitation was repeated from the door of the house; and Mrs. Price turned in, unprotesting and always sociably inclined, at the open gate.

## II.

It was a month later, and a whole autumn's length colder, when the two men were coming home from a long tramp through the woods. They had been making a solemn inspection of a wood-lot that they owned together, and had now visited their landmarks and outer boundaries, and settled the great question of cutting or not cutting some large pines. When it was well decided that a few years' growth would be no disadvantage to the timber, they had eaten an excellent cold luncheon and rested from their labors.

"I don't feel a day older 'n ever I did when I get out in the woods this way," announced John York, who was a prim, dusty-looking little man, a prudent person, who had been selectman of the town at least a dozen times.

"No more do I," agreed his companion, who was large and jovial and open-handed, more like a lucky sea-captain than a farmer. After pounding a slender walnut-tree with a heavy stone, he had succeeded in getting down a pocketful of late-hanging nuts which had escaped the squirrels, and was now snapping them back, one by one, to a venturesome chipmunk among some little frost-bitten beeches. Isaac Brown had a wonderfully pleasant way of getting on with all sorts of animals, even men. After a while they rose and went their way, these two companions, stopping here and there to look at a possible woodchuck's hole, or to strike a few hopeful blows at a hollow tree with the light axe which Isaac had carried to blaze new marks on some of the line-trees on the farther edge of their possessions. Sometimes they stopped to admire the size of an old hemlock, or to talk about thinning out the young pines. At last they were not very far from the entrance to the great tract of woodland. The yellow sunshine came slanting in much brighter against the tall trunks, spotting them with golden light high among the still branches.

Presently they came to a great ledge, frost-split and cracked into mysterious crevices.

"Here's where we used to get all the coons," said John York. "I haven't seen a coon this great while, spite o' your courage knocking on the trees up back here. You know that night we got the four fat ones? We started 'em somewheres near here, so the dog could get after 'em when they come out at night to go foragin'."

"Hold on, John;" and Mr. Isaac Brown got up from the log where he had just sat down to rest, and went to the ledge, and looked carefully all about. When he came back he was much excited, and beckoned his friend away, speaking in a stage whisper.

"I guess you'll see a coon before you're much older," he proclaimed. "I've thought it looked lately as if there'd been one about my place, and there's plenty o' signs here, right in their old haunts. Couple o' hens' heads an' a lot o' feathers" —

"Might be a fox," interrupted John York.

"Might be a coon," answered Mr. Isaac Brown. "I'm goin' to have him, too. I've been lookin' at every old hollow tree I passed, but I never thought o' this place. We 'll come right off to-morrow night, I guess, John, an' see if we can't get him. 'T is an extra handy place for 'em to den; in old times the folks always called it a good place; they 've been so sca'ce o' these late years that I 've thought little about 'em. Nothin' I ever liked so well as a coon-hunt. Gorry! he must be a big old fellow, by his tracks! See here, in this smooth dirt; just like a baby's footmark."

"Trouble is, we lack a good dog," said John York anxiously, after he had made an eager inspection. "I don't know where in the world to get one, either. There ain't no such a dog about as your Rover, but you 've let him get spoilt; these days I don't see him leave the yard. You ought to keep the women folks from overfeedin' of him so. He ought to 've lasted a good spell longer. He 's no use for huntin' now, that 's certain."

Isaac accepted the rebuke meekly. John York was a calm man, but he now grew very fierce under such a provocation. Nobody likes to be hindered in a coon-hunt.

"Oh, Rover 's too old, anyway," explained the affectionate master regretfully. "I 've been wishing all this afternoon I'd brought him; but I did n't think anything about him as we came away, I've got so used to seeing him layin' about the yard. 'T would have been a real treat for old Rover, if he could have kept up. Used to be at my heels the whole time. He could n't follow us, anyway, up here."

"I should n't wonder if he could," insisted John, with a humorous glance at his old friend, who was much too heavy and huge of girth for quick transit over rough ground. John York himself had grown lighter as he had grown older.

"I'll tell you one thing we could do," he hastened to suggest. "There's that dog of 'Bijah Topliff's. Don't you know the old lady told us, that day she went over to Dipford, how high he was valued? Most o' 'Bijah's important business was done in the fall, goin' out by night, gunning with fellows from the mills. He was just the kind of a worthless do-nothing that's sure to have an extra knowin' smart dog. I expect 'Liza Jane's got him now. Perhaps we could get him by to-morrow night. Let one o' my boys go over!"

"Why, 'Liza Jane's come, bag an' baggage, to spend the winter with her mother," exclaimed Isaac Brown, springing to his feet like a boy. " I 've had it in mind to tell you two or three times this afternoon, and then something else has flown it out of my head. I let my John Henry take the long-tailed wagon an' go down to the depot this mornin' to fetch her an' her goods up. The old lady come in early, while we were to breakfast, and to hear her lofty talk you 'd thought 't would taken a couple o' four-horse teams to move her. I told John Henry he might take that wagon and fetch up what light stuff he could, and see how much else there was, an' then I 'd make further arrangements. She said 'Liza Jane 'd see me well satisfied, an' rode off, pleased to death. I see 'em returnin' about eight, after the train was in. They 'd got 'Liza Jane with 'em, smaller 'n ever; and there was a trunk tied up with a rope, and a small roll o' beddin' and braided mats, and a quilted rockin'-chair. The old lady was holdin' on tight to a bird-cage with nothin' in it. Yes; an' I see the dog, too, in behind. He appeared kind of timid. He 's a yaller dog, but he ain't stump-tailed. They hauled up out front o' the house, and mother an' I went right out; Mis' Price always expects to have notice taken. She was in great sperits. Said 'Liza Jane concluded to sell off most of her stuff rather 'n have the care of it. She 'd told the folks that Mis' Topliff had a beautiful sofa and a lot o' nice chairs, and two framed pictures that would fix up the house complete, and invited us all to come over and see 'em. There, she seemed just as pleased returnin' with the bird-cage. Disappointments don't appear to trouble her no more than a butterfly. I kind of like the old creatur'; I don't mean to see her want."

"They 'll let us have the dog," said John York. "I don't know but I 'll give a quarter for him, and we 'll let 'em have a good piece o' the coon."

"You really comin' 'way up here by night, coon-huntin'?" asked Isaac Brown, looking reproachfully at his more agile comrade.

"I be," answered John York.

"I was dre'tful afraid you was only talking, and might back out," returned the cheerful heavy-weight, with a chuckle. "Now we 've got things all fixed, I feel more like it than ever. I tell you there 's just boy enough left inside of me. I 'll clean up my old gun to-morrow mornin', and you look right after your'n. I dare say the boys have took good care of 'em for us, but they don't know what we do about huntin', and we'll bring 'em all along and show 'em a little fun."

"All right," said John York, as soberly as if they were going to look after a piece of business for the town; and they gathered up the axe and other light possessions, and started toward home.

## III.

The two friends, whether by accident or design, came out of the woods some distance from their own houses, but very near to the low-storied little gray dwelling of Mrs. Price. They crossed the pasture, and climbed over the toppling fence at the foot of her small sandy piece of land, and knocked at the door. There was a light already in the kitchen. Mrs. Price and Eliza Jane Topliff appeared at once, eagerly hospitable.

"Anybody sick?" asked Mrs. Price, with instant sympathy. "Nothin' happened, I hope?"

"Oh, no," said both the men.

"We came to talk about hiring your dog

## THE COON DOG.

to-morrow night," explained Isaac Brown, feeling for the moment amused at his eager errand. " We got on track of a coon just now, up in the woods, and we thought we 'd give our boys a little treat. You shall have fifty cents, an' welcome, and a good piece o' the coon."

" Yes, Square Brown; we can let you have the dog as well as not," interrupted Mrs. Price, delighted to grant a favor. " Poor departed 'Bijah, he set everything by him as a coon dog. He always said a dog's capital was all in his reputation."

" You 'll have to be dreadful careful an' not lose him," urged Mrs. Topliff. " Yes, sir; he 's a proper coon dog as ever walked the earth, but he 's terrible weak-minded about followin' 'most anybody. 'Bijah used to travel off twelve or fourteen miles after him to git him back, when he wa'n't able. Somebody 'd speak to him decent, or fling a whip-lash as they drove by, an' off he 'd canter on three legs right after the wagon. But 'Bijah said he would n't trade him for no coon dog he ever was acquainted with. Trouble is, coons is awful sca'ce."

" I guess he ain't out o' practice," said John York amiably; " I guess he 'll know when he strikes the coon. Come, Isaac, we must be gittin' along tow'ds home. I feel like eatin' a good supper. You tie him up to-morrow afternoon, so we shall be sure to have him," he turned to say to Mrs. Price, who stood smiling at the door.

"Land sakes, dear, he won't git away; you'll find him right there betwixt the wood-box and the stove, where he is now. Hold the light, 'Liza Jane; they can't see their way out to the road. I'll fetch him over to ye in good season," she called out, by way of farewell; "'t will save ye third of a mile extra walk. No, 'Liza Jane; you'll let me do it, if you please. I've got a mother's heart. The gentlemen will excuse us for showin' feelin'. You're all the child I've got, an' your prosperity is the same as mine."

## IV.

The great night of the coon-hunt was frosty and still, with only a dim light from the new moon. John York and his boys, and Isaac Brown, whose excitement was very great, set forth across the fields toward the dark woods. The men seemed younger and gayer than the boys. There was a burst of laughter when John Henry Brown and his little brother appeared with the coon dog of the late Mr. Abijah Topliff, which had promptly run away home again after Mrs. Price had coaxed him over in the afternoon. The captors had tied a string round his neck, at which they pulled vigorously from time to time to urge him forward. Perhaps he found the night too cold; at any rate, he stopped short in the frozen furrows every few minutes, lifting one foot and whining a little. Half a dozen times he came near to tripping up Mr. Isaac Brown and making him fall at full length.

"Poor Tiger! poor Tiger!" said the good-natured sportsman, when somebody said that the dog did n't act as if he were much used to being out by night. "He 'll be all right when he once gets track of the coon." But when they were fairly in the woods, Tiger's distress was perfectly genuine. The long rays of light from the old-fashioned lanterns of pierced tin went wheeling round and round, making a tall ghost of every tree, and strange shadows went darting in and out behind the pines. The woods were like an interminable pillared room where the darkness made a high ceiling. The clean frosty smell of the open fields was changed for a warmer air, damp with the heavy odor of moss and fallen leaves. There was something wild and delicious in the forest in that hour of night. The men and boys tramped on silently in single file, as if they followed the flickering light instead of carrying it. The dog fell back by instinct, as did his companions, into the easy familiarity of forest life. He ran beside them, and watched eagerly as they chose a safe place to leave a coat or two and a basket. He seemed to be an affectionate dog, now that he had made acquaintance with his masters.

"Seems to me he don't exactly know what he 's about," said one of the York boys scornfully; "we must have struck that coon's track somewhere, comin' in."

"We 'll get through talkin', an' heap up a little somethin' for a fire, if you 'll turn to and help," said his father. "I 've always noticed that nobody can give so much good advice about a piece o' work as a new hand. When you 've treed as many coons as your Uncle Brown an' me, you won't feel so certain. Isaac, you be the one to take the dog up round the ledge, there. He 'll scent the

## THE COON DOG. 187

coon quick enough then. We'll 'tend to this part o' the business."

"You may come too, John Henry," said the indulgent father, and they set off together silently with the coon dog. He followed well enough now; his tail and ears were drooping even more than usual, but he whimpered along as bravely as he could, much excited, at John Henry's heels, like one of those great soldiers who are all unnerved until the battle is well begun.

A minute later the father and son came hurrying back, breathless, and stumbling over roots and bushes. The fire was already lighted, and sending a great glow higher and higher among the trees.

"He's off! He's struck a track! He was off like a major!" wheezed Mr. Isaac Brown.

"Which way 'd he go?" asked everybody.

"Right out toward the fields. Like's not the old fellow was just starting after more of our fowls. I'm glad we come early, — he can't have got far yet. We can't do nothin' but wait now, boys. I'll set right down here."

"Soon as the coon trees, you'll hear the

dog sing, now I tell you!" said John York, with great enthusiasm. "That night your father an' me got those four busters we've told you about, they come right back here to the ledge. I don't know but they will now. 'T was a dreadful cold night, I know. We did n't get home till past three o'clock in the mornin', either. You remember, don't you, Isaac?"

"I do," said Isaac. "How old Rover worked that night! Could n't see out of his eyes, nor hardly wag his clever old tail, for two days; thorns in both his fore paws, and the last coon took a piece right out of his off shoulder."

"Why did n't you let Rover come to-night, father?" asked the younger boy. "I think he knew somethin' was up. He was jumpin' round at a great rate when I come out of the yard."

"I did n't know but he might make trouble for the other dog," answered Isaac, after a moment's silence. He felt almost disloyal to the faithful creature, and had been missing him all the way. "'Sh! there's a bark!" And they all stopped to listen.

The fire was leaping higher; they all sat near it, listening and talking by turns.

There is apt to be a good deal of waiting in a coon-hunt.

"If Rover was young as he used to be, I'd resk him to tree any coon that ever run," said the regretful master. "This smart creature o' Topliff's can't beat him, I know. The poor old fellow's eyesight seems to be going. Two — three times he's run out at me right in broad day, an' barked when I come up the yard toward the house, and I did pity him dreadfully; he was so 'shamed when he found out what he'd done. Rover's a dog that's got an awful lot o' pride. He went right off out behind the long barn the last time, and wouldn't come in for nobody when they called him to supper till I went out myself and made it up with him. No; he can't see very well now, Rover can't."

"He's heavy, too; he's got too unwieldy to tackle a smart coon, I expect, even if he could do the tall runnin'," said John York, with sympathy. "They have to get a master grip with their teeth through a coon's thick pelt this time o' year. No; the young folks gets all the good chances after a while;" and he looked round indulgently at the chubby faces of his boys, who fed the fire, and rejoiced in being promoted to the society of their elders on equal terms. "Ain't it time we heard from the dog?" And they all listened, while the fire snapped and the sap whistled in some green sticks.

"I hear him," said John Henry suddenly; and faint and far away there came the sound of a desperate bark. There is a bark that means attack, and there is a bark that means only foolish excitement.

"They ain't far off!" said Isaac. "My gracious, he's right after him! I don't know's I expected that poor-looking dog to be so smart. You can't tell by their looks. Quick as he scented the game up here in the rocks, off he put. Perhaps it ain't any matter if they ain't stump-tailed, long's they 're yaller dogs. He did n't look heavy enough to me. I tell you, he means business. Hear that bark!"

"They all bark alike after a coon." John York was as excited as anybody. "Git the guns laid out to hand, boys; I told you we 'd ought to follow!" he commanded. "If it 's the old fellow that belongs here, he may put in any minute." But there was again a long silence and state of suspense; the chase had turned another way. There were faint distant yaps. The fire burned low and fell together with a shower of sparks. The smaller boys began to grow chilly and sleepy, when there was a thud and rustle and snapping of twigs close at hand, then the gasp of a breathless dog. Two dim shapes rushed by; a shower of bark fell, and a dog began to sing at the foot of the great twisted pine not fifty feet away.

"Hooray for Tiger!" yelled the boys; but the dog's voice filled all the woods. It might have echoed to the mountain-tops. There was the old coon; they could all see him half-way up the tree, flat to the great limb. They heaped the fire with dry branches till it flared high. Now they lost him in a shadow as he twisted about the tree. John York fired, and Isaac Brown fired, and the boys took a turn at the guns, while John Henry started to climb a neighboring oak; but at last it was Isaac who brought the coon to ground with a lucky shot, and the dog stopped his deafening bark and frantic leaping in the underbrush, and after an astonishing moment of silence crept out, a proud victor, to his prouder master's feet.

"Goodness alive, who's this? Good for

you, old handsome! Why, I'll be hanged if it ain't old Rover, boys; *it's old Rover!*" But Isaac could not speak another word. They all crowded round the wistful, clumsy old dog, whose eyes shone bright, though his breath was all gone. Each man patted him, and praised him, and said they ought to have mistrusted all the time that it could be nobody but he. It was some minutes before Isaac Brown could trust himself to do anything but pat the sleek old head that was always ready to his hand.

"He must have overheard us talkin'; I guess he'd have come if he'd dropped dead half-way," proclaimed John Henry, like a prince of the reigning house; and Rover wagged his tail as if in honest assent, as he lay at his master's side. They sat together, while the fire was brightened again to make a good light for the coon-hunt supper; and Rover had a good half of everything that found its way into his master's hand. It was toward midnight when the triumphal procession set forth toward home, with the two lanterns, across the fields.

## V.

The next morning was bright and warm after the hard frost of the night before. Old Rover was asleep on the doorstep in the sun, and his master stood in the yard, and saw neighbor Price come along the road in her best array, with a gay holiday air.

"Well, now," she said eagerly, "you wa'n't out very late last night, was you? I got up myself to let Tiger in. He come home, all beat out, about a quarter past nine. I expect you had n't no kind o' trouble gittin' the coon. The boys was tellin' me he weighed 'most thirty pounds."

"Oh, no kind o' trouble," said Isaac, keeping the great secret gallantly. "You got the things I sent over this mornin'?"

"Bless your heart, yes! I'd a sight rather have all that good pork an' potatoes than any o' your wild meat," said Mrs. Price, smiling with prosperity. "You see, now, 'Liza Jane she's given in. She did n't re'lly know but 't was all talk of 'Bijah 'bout that dog's bein' wuth fifty dollars. She says she can't cope with a huntin' dog same 's he could, an' she's given me the money you an' John York sent over this mornin'; an' I did n't know but what you 'd lend me another half a dollar, so I could both go to Dipford Centre an' return, an' see if I could n't make a sale o' Tiger right over there where they all know about him. It's right in the coon season; now 's my time, ain't it?"

"Well, gettin' a little late," said Isaac, shaking with laughter as he took the desired sum of money out of his pocket. "He seems to be a clever dog round the house."

"I don't know 's I want to harbor him all winter," answered the excursionist frankly, striking into a good traveling gait as she started off toward the railroad station.

# AUNT CYNTHY DALLETT.

## I.

"No," said Mrs. Hand, speaking wistfully, — " no, we never were in the habit of keeping Christmas at our house. Mother died when we were all young; she would have been the one to keep up with all new ideas, but father and grandmother were old-fashioned folks, and — well, you know how 't was then, Miss Pendexter: nobody took much notice of the day except to wish you a Merry Christmas."

"They did n't do much to make it merry, certain," answered Miss Pendexter. "Sometimes nowadays I hear folks complainin' o' bein' overtaxed with all the Christmas work they have to do."

"Well, others think that it makes a lovely chance for all that really enjoys givin'; you get an opportunity to speak your kind feelin' right out," answered Mrs. Hand, with a bright smile. "But there! I shall always keep New Year's Day, too; it won't do no hurt to have an extra day kept an' made pleasant. And there's many of the real old folks have got pretty things to remember about New Year's Day."

"Aunt Cynthy Dallett's just one of 'em," said Miss Pendexter. "She's always very reproachful if I don't get up to see her. Last year I missed it, on account of a light fall o' snow that seemed to make the walkin' too bad, an' she sent a neighbor's boy 'way down from the mount'in to see if I was sick. Her lameness confines her to the house altogether now, an' I have her on my mind a good deal. How anybody does get thinkin' of those that lives alone, as they get older! I waked up only last night with a start, thinkin' if Aunt Cynthy's house should get afire or anything, what she would do, 'way up there all alone. I was half dreamin', I s'pose, but I couldn't seem to settle down until I got up an' went upstairs to the north garret window to see if I could see any light; but the mountains was all dark an' safe, same's usual. I remember noticin' last time I was there that her chimney needed pointin', and I spoke to her about it, — the bricks looked poor in some places."

"Can you see the house from your north

gable window?" asked Mrs. Hand, a little absently.

"Yes 'm; it's a great comfort that I can," answered her companion. "I have often wished we were near enough to have her make me some sort o' signal in case she needed help. I used to plead with her to come down and spend the winters with me, but she told me one day I might as well try to fetch down one o' the old hemlocks, an' I believe 't was true."

"Your aunt Dallett is a very self-contained person," observed Mrs. Hand.

"Oh, very!" exclaimed the elderly niece, with a pleased look. "Aunt Cynthy laughs, an' says she expects the time will come when age 'll compel her to have me move up an' take care of her; and last time I was there she looked up real funny, an' says, 'I do' know, Abby; I'm most afeard sometimes that I feel myself beginnin' to look for'ard to it!' 'T was a good deal, comin' from Aunt Cynthy, an' I so esteemed it."

"She ought to have you there now," said Mrs. Hand. "You'd both make a savin' by doin' it; but I don't expect she needs to save as much as some. There! I know just how you both feel. I like to have my own home an' do everything just my way too." And the friends laughed, and looked at each other affectionately.

"There was old Mr. Nathan Dunn, — left no debts an' no money when he died," said Mrs. Hand. "'T was over to his niece's last summer. He had a little money in his wallet, an' when the bill for funeral expenses come in there was just exactly enough; some item or other made it come to so many dollars an' eighty-four cents, and, lo an' behold! there was eighty-four cents in a little separate pocket beside the neat fold o' bills, as if the old gentleman had known beforehand. His niece could n't help laughin', to save her; she said the old gentleman died as methodical as he lived. She did n't expect he had any money, an' was prepared to pay for everything herself; she 's very well off."

"'T was funny, certain," said Miss Pendexter. "I expect he felt comfortable, knowin' he had that money by him. 'T is a comfort, when all 's said and done, 'specially to folks that 's gettin' old."

A sad look shadowed her face for an instant, and then she smiled and rose to take leave, looking expectantly at her hostess to see if there were anything more to be said.

"I hope to come out square myself," she said, by way of farewell pleasantry; "but there are times when I feel doubtful."

Mrs. Hand was evidently considering something, and waited a moment or two before she spoke. "Suppose we both walk up to see your aunt Dallett, New Year's Day, if it ain't too windy and the snow keeps off?" she proposed. "I could n't rise the hill if 't was a windy day. We could take a hearty breakfast an' start in good season; I 'd rather walk than ride, the road 's so rough this time o' year."

"Oh, what a person you are to think o' things! I did so dread goin' 'way up there all alone," said Abby Pendexter. "I 'm no hand to go off alone, an' I had it before me, so I really got to dread it. I do so enjoy it after I get there, seein' Aunt Cynthy, an' she 's always so much better than I expect to find her."

"Well, we 'll start early," said Mrs. Hand cheerfully; and so they parted. As Miss Pendexter went down the foot-path to the gate, she sent grateful thoughts back to the little sitting-room she had just left.

"How doors are opened!" she exclaimed to herself. "Here I 've been so poor an' distressed at beginnin' the year with nothin', as it were, that I could n't think o' even goin' to make poor old Aunt Cynthy a friendly call. I 'll manage to make some kind of a little pleasure too, an' somethin' for dear Mis' Hand. 'Use what you 've got,' mother always used to say when every sort of an emergency come up, an' I may only have wishes to give, but I 'll make 'em good ones!"

## II.

The first day of the year was clear and bright, as if it were a New Year's pattern of what winter can be at its very best. The two friends were prepared for changes of weather, and met each other well wrapped in their winter cloaks and shawls, with sufficient brown barége veils tied securely over their bonnets. They ignored for some time the plain truth that each carried something under her arm; the shawls were rounded out suspiciously, especially Miss Pendexter's, but each respected the other's air of secrecy. The narrow road was frozen in deep ruts, but a smooth-trodden little foot-path that ran along its edge was very inviting to the wayfarers. Mrs. Hand walked first and

Miss Pendexter followed, and they were talking busily nearly all the way, so that they had to stop for breath now and then at the tops of the little hills. It was not a hard walk; there were a good many almost level stretches through the woods, in spite of the fact that they should be a very great deal higher when they reached Mrs. Dallett's door.

"I do declare, what a nice day 't is, an' such pretty footin'!" said Mrs. Hand, with satisfaction. "Seems to me as if my feet went o' themselves; gener'lly I have to toil so when I walk that I can't enjoy nothin' when I get to a place."

"It 's partly this beautiful bracin' air," said Abby Pendexter. "Sometimes such nice air comes just before a fall of snow. Don't it seem to make anybody feel young again and to take all your troubles away?"

Mrs. Hand was a comfortable, well-to-do soul, who seldom worried about anything, but something in her companion's tone touched her heart, and she glanced sidewise and saw a pained look in Abby Pendexter's thin face. It was a moment for confidence.

"Why, you speak as if something distressed your mind, Abby," said the elder woman kindly.

"I ain't one that has myself on my mind as a usual thing, but it does seem now as if I was goin' to have it very hard," said Abby. "Well, I've been anxious before."

"Is it anything wrong about your property?" Mrs. Hand ventured to ask.

"Only that I ain't got any," answered Abby, trying to speak gayly. "'T was all I could do to pay my last quarter's rent, twelve dollars. I sold my hens, all but this one that had run away at the time, an' now I'm carryin' her up to Aunt Cynthy, roasted just as nice as I know how."

"I thought you was carrying somethin'," said Mrs. Hand, in her usual tone. "For me, I've got a couple o' my mince pies. I thought the old lady might like 'em; one we can eat for our dinner, and one she shall have to keep. But were n't you unwise to sacrifice your poultry, Abby? You always need eggs, and hens don't cost much to keep."

"Why, yes, I shall miss 'em," said Abby; "but, you see, I had to do every way to get my rent-money. Now the shop's shut down I have n't got any way of earnin' anything, and I spent what little I've saved through the summer."

"Your aunt Cynthy ought to know it

an' ought to help you," said Mrs. Hand. "You're a real foolish person, I must say. I expect you do for her when she ought to do for you."

"She's old, an' she's all the near relation I've got," said the little woman. "I've always felt the time would come when she'd need me, but it's been her great pleasure to live alone an' feel free. I shall get along somehow, but I shall have it hard. Somebody may want help for a spell this winter, but I'm afraid I shall have to give up my house. 'T ain't as if I owned it. I don't know just what to do, but there'll be a way."

Mrs. Hand shifted her two pies to the other arm, and stepped across to the other side of the road where the ground looked a little smoother.

"No, I wouldn't worry if I was you, Abby," she said. "There, I suppose if 't was me I should worry a good deal more! I expect I should lay awake nights." But Abby answered nothing, and they came to a steep place in the road and found another subject for conversation at the top.

"Your aunt don't know we're coming?" asked the chief guest of the occasion.

"Oh, no, I never send her word," said

Miss Pendexter. "She'd be so desirous to get everything ready, just as she used to."

"She never seemed to make any trouble o' havin' company; she always appeared so easy and pleasant, and let you set with her while she made her preparations," said Mrs. Hand, with great approval. "Some has such a dreadful way of making you feel inopportune, and you can't always send word you're comin'. I did have a visit once that's always been a lesson to me; 't was years ago; I don't know 's I ever told you?"

"I don't believe you ever did," responded the listener to this somewhat indefinite prelude.

"Well, 't was one hot summer afternoon. I set forth an' took a great long walk 'way over to Mis' Eben Fulham's, on the crossroad between the cranberry ma'sh and Staples's Corner. The doctor was drivin' that way, an' he give me a lift that shortened it some at the last; but I never should have started, if I'd known 't was so far. I had been promisin' all summer to go, and every time I saw Mis' Fulham, Sundays, she'd say somethin' about it. We wa'n't very well acquainted, but always friendly. She moved here from Bedford Hill."

## AUNT CYNTHY DALLETT.   205

"Oh, yes; I used to know her," said Abby, with interest.

"Well, now, she did give me a beautiful welcome when I got there," continued Mrs. Hand. "'T was about four o'clock in the afternoon, an' I told her I 'd come to accept her invitation if 't was convenient, an' the doctor had been called several miles beyond and expected to be detained, but he was goin' to pick me up as he returned about seven; 't was very kind of him. She took me right in, and she did appear so pleased, an' I must go right into the best room where 't was cool, and then she said she 'd have tea early, and I should have to excuse her a short time. I asked her not to make any difference, and if I could n't assist her; but she said no, I must just take her as I found her; and she give me a large fan, and off she went.

"There. I was glad to be still and rest where 't was cool, an' I set there in the rockin'-chair an' enjoyed it for a while, an' I heard her clacking at the oven door out beyond, an' gittin' out some dishes. She was a brisk-actin' little woman, an' I thought I 'd caution her when she come back not to make up a great fire, only for a cup o' tea, perhaps. I started to go right out in the kitchen, an' then somethin' told me I'd better not, we never'd been so free together as that; I didn't know how she'd take it, an' there I set an' set. 'T was sort of a greenish light in the best room, an' it begun to feel a little damp to me, — the s'rubs outside grew close up to the windows. Oh, it did seem dreadful long! I could hear her busy with the dishes an' beatin' eggs an' stirrin', an' I knew she was puttin' herself out to get up a great supper, and I kind o' fidgeted about a little an' even stepped to the door, but I thought she'd expect me to remain where I was. I saw everything in that room forty times over, an' I did divert myself killin' off a brood o' moths that was in a worsted-work mat on the table. It all fell to pieces. I never saw such a sight o' moths to once. But occupation failed after that, an' I begun to feel sort o' tired an' numb. There was one o' them late crickets got into the room an' begun to chirp, an' it sounded kind o' fallish. I couldn't help sayin' to myself that Mis' Fulham had forgot all about my bein' there. I thought of all the beauties of hospitality that ever I see!" —

"Didn't she ever come back at all, not whilst things was in the oven, nor nothin'?" inquired Miss Pendexter, with awe.

"I never see her again till she come beamin' to the parlor door an' invited me to walk out to tea," said Mrs. Hand. "'T was 'most a quarter past six by the clock; I thought 't was seven. I'd thought o' everything, an' I'd counted, an' I'd trotted my foot, an' I'd looked more 'n twenty times to see if there was any more moth-millers."

"I s'pose you did have a very nice tea?" suggested Abby, with interest.

"Oh, a beautiful tea! She could n't have done more if I'd been the Queen," said Mrs. Hand. "I don't know how she could ever have done it all in the time, I'm sure. The table was loaded down; there was cup-custards and custard pie, an' cream pie, an' two kinds o' hot biscuits, an' black tea as well as green, an' elegant cake, — one kind she 'd just made new, and called it quick cake; I've often made it since — an' she 'd opened her best preserves, two kinds. We set down together, an' I'm sure I appreciated what she 'd done; but 't wa'n't no time for real conversation whilst we was to the table, and before we got quite through the doctor come hurryin' along, an' I had to leave. He asked us if we 'd had a good talk, as we come out, an' I could n't help laughing to myself; but she said quite hearty that she'd had a nice visit from me. She appeared well satisfied, Mis' Fulham did; but for me, I was disappointed; an' early that fall she died."

Abby Pendexter was laughing like a girl; the speaker's tone had grown more and more complaining. "I do call that a funny experience," she said. "'Better a dinner o' herbs.' I guess that text must ha' risen to your mind in connection. You must tell that to Aunt Cynthy, if conversation seems to fail." And she laughed again, but Mrs. Hand still looked solemn and reproachful.

"Here we are; there's Aunt Cynthy's lane right ahead, there by the great yellow birch," said Abby. "I must say, you've made the way seem very short, Mis' Hand."

### III.

Old Aunt Cynthia Dallett sat in her high-backed rocking-chair by the little north window, which was her favorite dwelling-place.

"New Year's Day again," she said, aloud, — "New Year's Day again!" And she folded her old bent hands, and looked out at the great woodland view and the hills without really seeing them, she was lost in so deep a reverie. "I 'm gittin' to be very old," she added, after a little while.

It was perfectly still in the small gray house. Outside in the apple-trees there were some blue-jays flitting about and calling noisily, like schoolboys fighting at their games. The kitchen was full of pale winter sunshine. It was more like late October than the first of January, and the plain little room seemed to smile back into the sun's face. The outer door was standing open into the green dooryard, and a fat small dog lay asleep on the step. A capacious cupboard stood behind Mrs. Dallett's chair and kept the wind away from her corner. Its doors and drawers were painted a clean lead-color, and there were places round the knobs and buttons where the touch of hands had worn deep into the wood. Every braided rug was straight on the floor. The square clock on its shelf between the front windows looked as if it had just had its face washed and been wound up for a whole year to come. If Mrs. Dallett turned her head she could look into the bedroom, where her plump feather bed was covered with its dark blue homespun winter quilt. It was all very peaceful and comfortable, but it was very lonely. By her side, on a light-stand, lay the religious newspaper of her denomination, and a pair of spectacles whose jointed silver bows looked like a funny two-legged beetle cast helplessly upon its back.

"New Year's Day again," said old Cynthia Dallett. Time had left nobody in her house to wish her a Happy New Year, — she was the last one left in the old nest. "I'm gittin' to be very old," she said for the second time; it seemed to be all there was to say.

She was keeping a careful eye on her friendly clock, but it was hardly past the middle of the morning, and there was no excuse for moving; it was the long hour between the end of her slow morning work and the appointed time for beginning to get dinner. She was so stiff and lame that this hour's rest was usually most welcome, but to-day she sat as if it were Sunday, and did not take up her old shallow splint basket of braiding-rags from the side of her footstool.

"I do hope Abby Pendexter 'll make out to git up to see me this afternoon as usual," she continued. "I know 't ain't so easy for her to get up the hill as it used to be, but I do seem to want to see some o' my own folks. I wish 't I 'd thought to send her word I expected her when Jabez Hooper went back after he came up here with the flour. I 'd like to have had her come prepared to stop two or three days."

A little chickadee perched on the window-sill outside and bobbed his head sideways to look in, and then pecked impatiently at the glass. The old woman laughed at him with childish pleasure and felt companioned; it was pleasant at that moment to see the life in even a bird's bright eye.

"Sign of a stranger," she said, as he whisked his wings and flew away in a hurry. "I must throw out some crumbs for 'em; it's getting to be hard pickin' for the stayin'-birds." She looked past the trees of her little orchard now with seeing eyes, and followed the long forest slopes that led downward to the lowland country. She could see the two white steeples of Fairfield Village, and the map of fields and pastures along the valley beyond, and the great hills across the valley to the westward. The scattered houses looked like toys that had been scattered by children. She knew their lights by night, and watched the smoke of their chimneys by day. Far to the northward were higher mountains, and these were already white with snow. Winter was already in sight, but to-day the wind was in the south, and the snow seemed only part of a great picture.

"I do hope the cold 'll keep off a while longer," thought Mrs. Dallett. "I don't know how I'm going to get along after the deep snow comes."

The little dog suddenly waked, as if he had had a bad dream, and after giving a few anxious whines he began to bark outrageously. His mistress tried, as usual, to appeal to his better feelings.

"'T ain't nobody, Tiger," she said. "Can't you have some patience? Maybe it's some foolish boys that's rangin' about with their guns." But Tiger kept on, and even took the trouble to waddle in on his short legs, barking all the way. He looked warningly at her, and then turned and ran out again. Then she saw him go hurrying down to the bars, as if it were an occasion of unusual interest.

"I guess somebody is comin'; he don't act as if 't were a vagrant kind o' noise; must really be somebody in our lane." And

Mrs. Dallett smoothed her apron and gave an anxious housekeeper's glance round the kitchen. None of her state visitors, the minister or the deacons, ever came in the morning. Country people are usually too busy to go visiting in the forenoons.

Presently two figures appeared where the road came out of the woods, — the two women already known to the story, but very surprising to Mrs. Dallett; the short, thin one was easily recognized as Abby Pendexter, and the taller, stout one was soon discovered to be Mrs. Hand. Their old friend's heart was in a glow. As the guests approached they could see her pale face with its thin white hair framed under the close black silk handkerchief.

"There she is at her window smilin' away!" exclaimed Mrs. Hand; but by the time they reached the doorstep she stood waiting to meet them.

"Why, you two dear creatur's!" she said, with a beaming smile. "I don't know when I've ever been so glad to see folks comin'. I had a kind of left-all-alone feelin' this mornin', an' I didn't even make bold to be certain o' you, Abby, though it looked so pleasant. Come right in an' set down.

You're all out o' breath, ain't you, Mis' Hand?"

Mrs. Dallett led the way with eager hospitality. She was the tiniest little bent old creature, her handkerchiefed head was quick and alert, and her eyes were bright with excitement and feeling, but the rest of her was much the worse for age; she could hardly move, poor soul, as if she had only a make-believe framework of a body under a shoulder-shawl and thick petticoats. She got back to her chair again, and the guests took off their bonnets in the bedroom, and returned discreet and sedate in their black woolen dresses. The lonely kitchen was blest with society at last, to its mistress's heart's content. They talked as fast as possible about the weather, and how warm it had been walking up the mountain, and how cold it had been a year ago, that day when Abby Pendexter had been kept at home by a snowstorm and missed her visit. "And I ain't seen you now, aunt, since the twenty-eighth of September, but I've thought of you a great deal, and looked forward to comin' more 'n usual," she ended, with an affectionate glance at the pleased old face by the window.

"I've been wantin' to see you, dear, and wonderin' how you was gettin' on," said Aunt Cynthy kindly. "And I take it as a great attention to have you come to-day, Mis' Hand," she added, turning again towards the more distinguished guest. "We have to put one thing against another. I should hate dreadfully to live anywhere except on a high hill farm, 'cordin' as I was born an' raised. But there ain't the chance to neighbor that townfolks has, an' I do seem to have more lonely hours than I used to when I was younger. I don't know but I shall soon be gittin' too old to live alone." And she turned to her niece with an expectant, lovely look, and Abby smiled back.

"I often wish I could run in an' see you every day, aunt," she answered. "I have been sayin' so to Mrs. Hand."

"There, how anybody does relish company when they don't have but a little of it!" exclaimed Aunt Cynthia. "I am all alone to-day; there is going to be a shootin'-match somewhere the other side o' the mountain, an' Johnny Foss, that does my chores, begged off to go when he brought the milk unusual early this mornin'. Gener'lly he's about here all the fore part of the day; but he don't go off with the boys very often, and I like to have him have a little sport; 't was New Year's Day, anyway; he's a good, stiddy boy for my wants."

"Why, I wish you Happy New Year, aunt!" said Abby, springing up with unusual spirit. "Why, that's just what we come to say, and we like to have forgot all about it!" She kissed her aunt, and stood a minute holding her hand with a soft, affectionate touch. Mrs. Hand rose and kissed Mrs. Dallett too, and it was a moment of ceremony and deep feeling.

"I always like to keep the day," said the old hostess, as they seated themselves and drew their splint-bottomed chairs a little nearer together than before. "You see, I was brought up to it, and father made a good deal of it; he said he liked to make it pleasant and give the year a fair start. I can see him now, how he used to be standing there by the fireplace when we came out o' the two bedrooms early in the morning, an' he always made out, poor's he was, to give us some little present, and he'd heap 'em up on the corner o' the mantelpiece, an' we'd stand front of him in a row, and mother be bustling about gettin' breakfast.

One year he give me a beautiful copy o' the 'Life o' General Lafayette,' in a green cover, — I 've got it now, but we child'n 'bout read it to pieces, — an' one year a nice piece o' blue ribbon, an' Abby — that was your mother, Abby — had a pink one. Father was real kind to his child'n. I thought o' them early days when I first waked up this mornin', and I could n't help lookin' up then to the corner o' the shelf just as I used to look."

"There's nothin' so beautiful as to have a bright childhood to look back to," said Mrs. Hand. "Sometimes I think child'n has too hard a time now, — all the responsibility is put on to 'em, since they take the lead o' what to do an' what they want, and get to be so toppin' an' knowin'. 'T was happier in the old days, when the fathers an' mothers done the rulin'."

"They say things have changed," said Aunt Cynthy; "but staying right here, I don't know much of any world but my own world."

Abby Pendexter did not join in this conversation, but sat in her straight-backed chair with folded hands and the air of a good child. The little old dog had followed

her in, and now lay sound asleep again at
her feet. The front breadth of her black
dress looked rusty and old in the sunshine
that slanted across it, and the aunt's sharp
eyes saw this and saw the careful darns.
Abby was as neat as wax, but she looked as
if the frost had struck her. "I declare,
she's gittin' along in years," thought Aunt
Cynthia compassionately. "She begins to
look sort o' set and dried up, Abby does.
She ought n't to live all alone; she's one
that needs company."

At this moment Abby looked up with
new interest. "Now, aunt," she said, in her
pleasant voice, "I don't want you to forget
to tell me if there ain't some sewin' or
mendin' I can do whilst I'm here. I know
your hands trouble you some, an' I may's
well tell you we 're bent on stayin' all day
an' makin' a good visit, Mis' Hand an' me."

"Thank ye kindly," said the old woman;
"I do want a little sewin' done before long,
but 't ain't no use to spile a good holiday."
Her face took a resolved expression. "I'm
goin' to make other arrangements," she
said. "No, you need n't come up here to
pass New Year's Day an' be put right down
to sewin'. I make out to do what mendin'

I need, an' to sew on my hooks an' eyes. I get Johnny Ross to thread me up a good lot o' needles every little while, an' that helps me a good deal. Abby, why can't you step into the best room an' bring out the rockin'-chair? I seem to want Mis' Hand to have it."

"I opened the window to let the sun in awhile," said the niece, as she returned. "It felt cool in there an' shut up."

"I thought of doin' it not long before you come," said Mrs. Dallett, looking gratified. Once the taking of such a liberty would have been very provoking to her. "Why, it does seem good to have somebody think o' things an' take right hold like that!"

"I'm sure you would, if you were down at my house," said Abby, blushing. "Aunt Cynthy, I don't suppose you could feel as if 't would be best to come down an' pass the winter with me, — just durin' the cold weather, I mean. You'd see more folks to amuse you, an' — I do think of you so anxious these long winter nights."

There was a terrible silence in the room, and Miss Pendexter felt her heart begin to beat very fast. She did not dare to look at her aunt at first.

Presently the silence was broken. Aunt Cynthia had been gazing out of the window, and she turned towards them a little paler and older than before, and smiling sadly.

"Well, dear, I'll do just as you say," she answered. "I'm beat by age at last, but I've had my own way for eighty-five years, come the month o' March, an' last winter I did use to lay awake an' worry in the long storms. I'm kind o' humble now about livin' alone to what I was once." At this moment a new light shone in her face. "I don't expect you'd be willin' to come up here an' stay till spring,— not if I had Foss's folks stop for you to ride to meetin' every pleasant Sunday, an' take you down to the Corners plenty o' other times besides?" she said beseechingly. "No, Abby, I'm too old to move now; I should be homesick down to the village. If you'll come an' stay with me, all I have shall be yours. Mis' Hand hears me say it."

"Oh, don't you think o' that; you're all I've got near to me in the world, an' I'll come an' welcome," said Abby, though the thought of her own little home gave a hard tug at her heart. "Yes, Aunt Cynthy, I'll come, an' we'll be real comfortable together. I've been lonesome sometimes" —

"'T will be best for both," said Mrs. Hand judicially. And so the great question was settled, and suddenly, without too much excitement, it became a thing of the past.

"We must be thinkin' o' dinner," said Aunt Cynthia gayly. "I wish I was better prepared; but there's nice eggs an' pork an' potatoes, an' you girls can take hold an' help." At this moment the roast chicken and the best mince pies were offered and kindly accepted, and before another hour had gone they were sitting at their New Year feast, which Mrs. Dallett decided to be quite proper for the Queen.

Before the guests departed, when the sun was getting low, Aunt Cynthia called her niece to her side and took hold of her hand.

"Don't you make it too long now, Abby," said she. "I shall be wantin' ye every day till you come; but you mustn't forgit what a set old thing I be."

Abby had the kindest of hearts, and was always longing for somebody to love and care for; her aunt's very age and helplessness seemed to beg for pity.

"This is Saturday; you may expect me the early part of the week; and thank you, too, aunt," said Abby.

Mrs. Hand stood by with deep sympathy. "It's the proper thing," she announced calmly. "You'd both of you be a sight happier; and truth is, Abby's wild an' reckless, an' needs somebody to stand right over her, Mis' Dallett. I guess she'll try an' behave, but there — there's no knowin'!" And they all laughed. Then the New Year guests said farewell and started off down the mountain road. They looked back more than once to see Aunt Cynthia's face at the window as she watched them out of sight. Miss Abby Pendexter was full of excitement; she looked as happy as a child.

"I feel as if we'd gained the battle of Waterloo," said Mrs. Hand. "I've really had a most beautiful time. You an' your aunt must n't forgit to invite me up some time again to spend another day."

# THE NIGHT BEFORE THANKS-GIVING.

## I.

There was a sad heart in the low-storied, dark little house that stood humbly by the roadside under some tall elms. Small as her house was, old Mrs. Robb found it too large for herself alone; she only needed the kitchen and a tiny bedroom that led out of it, and there still remained the best room and a bedroom, with the low garret overhead.

There had been a time, after she was left alone, when Mrs. Robb could help those who were poorer than herself. She was strong enough not only to do a woman's work inside her house, but almost a man's work outside in her piece of garden ground. At last sickness and age had come hand in hand, those two relentless enemies of the poor, and together they had wasted her strength and substance. She had always been looked up to by her neighbors as being independent, but now she was left, lame-footed and lame-handed, with a debt to carry and her bare land, and the house ill-provisioned to stand the siege of time.

For a while she managed to get on, but at last it began to be whispered about that there was no use for any one so proud; it was easier for the whole town to care for her than for a few neighbors, and Mrs. Robb had better go to the poorhouse before winter, and be done with it. At this terrible suggestion her brave heart seemed to stand still. The people whom she cared for most happened to be poor, and she could no longer go into their households to make herself of use. The very elms overhead seemed to say, "Oh, no!" as they groaned in the late autumn winds, and there was something appealing even to the strange passer-by in the look of the little gray house, with Mrs. Robb's pale, worried face at the window.

## II.

Some one has said that anniversaries are days to make other people happy in, but sometimes when they come they seem to be full of shadows, and the power of giving joy to others, that inalienable right which ought to lighten the saddest heart, the most indifferent sympathy, sometimes even this seems to be withdrawn.

So poor old Mary Ann Robb sat at her window on the afternoon before Thanksgiving and felt herself poor and sorrowful indeed. Across the frozen road she looked eastward over a great stretch of cold meadow land, brown and wind-swept and crossed by icy ditches. It seemed to her as if before this, in all the troubles that she had known and carried, there had always been some hope to hold: as if she had never looked poverty full in the face and seen its cold and pitiless look before. She looked anxiously down the road, with a horrible shrinking and dread at the thought of being asked, out of pity, to join in some Thanksgiving feast, but there was nobody coming with gifts in hand. Once she had been full of love for such days, whether at home or abroad, but something chilled her very heart now.

Her nearest neighbor had been foremost of those who wished her to go to the town farm, and he had said more than once that it was the only sensible thing. But John Mander was waiting impatiently to get her tiny farm into his own hands; he had advanced some money upon it in her extremity, and pretended that there was still a debt, after he cleared her wood lot to pay himself back. He would plough over the graves in the field corner and fell the great elms, and waited now like a spider for his poor prey. He often reproached her for being too generous to worthless people in the past and coming to be a charge to others now. Oh, if she could only die in her own house and not suffer the pain of homelessness and dependence!

It was just at sunset, and as she looked out hopelessly across the gray fields, there was a sudden gleam of light far away on the low hills beyond; the clouds opened in the west and let the sunshine through. One lovely gleam shot swift as an arrow and brightened a far cold hillside where it fell, and at the same moment a sudden gleam of hope brightened the winter landscape of her heart.

"There was Johnny Harris," said Mary Ann Robb softly. "He was a soldier's son, left an orphan and distressed. Old John Mander scolded, but I could n't see the poor boy in want. I kept him that year after he got hurt, spite o' what anybody said, an' he helped me what little he could. He said I was the only mother he'd ever had. 'I'm goin' out West, Mother Robb,' says he. 'I sha'n't come back till I get rich,' an' then he'd look at me an' laugh, so pleasant and boyish. He wa'n't one that liked to write. I don't think he was doin' very well when I heard,— there, it's most four years ago now. I always thought if he got sick or anything, I should have a good home for him to come to. There's poor Ezra Blake, the deaf one, too,— he won't have any place to welcome him."

The light faded out of doors, and again Mrs. Robb's troubles stood before her. Yet it was not so dark as it had been in her sad heart. She still sat by the window, hoping now, in spite of herself, instead of fearing; and a curious feeling of nearness and expectancy made her feel not so much light-hearted as light-headed.

"I feel just as if somethin' was goin' to happen," she said. "Poor Johnny Harris, perhaps he's thinkin' o' me, if he's alive."

It was dark now out of doors, and there were tiny clicks against the window. It was beginning to snow, and the great elms creaked in the rising wind overhead.

## III.

A dead limb of one of the old trees had fallen that autumn, and, poor firewood as it might be, it was Mrs. Robb's own, and she had burnt it most thankfully. There was only a small armful left, but at least she could have the luxury of a fire. She had a feeling that it was her last night at home, and with strange recklessness began to fill the stove as she used to do in better days.

"It'll get me good an' warm," she said, still talking to herself, as lonely people do, "an' I'll go to bed early. It's comin' on to storm."

The snow clicked faster and faster against the window, and she sat alone thinking in the dark.

"There's lots of folks I love," she said once. "They'd be sorry I ain't got nobody to come, an' no supper the night afore Thanksgivin'. I'm dreadful glad they don't know." And she drew a little nearer to the fire, and laid her head back drowsily in the old rocking-chair.

It seemed only a moment before there was a loud knocking, and somebody lifted the latch of the door. The fire shone bright through the front of the stove and made a little light in the room, but Mary Ann Robb waked up frightened and bewildered.

"Who's there?" she called, as she found her crutch and went to the door. She was only conscious of her one great fear. "They've come to take me to the poorhouse!" she said, and burst into tears.

There was a tall man, not John Mander, who seemed to fill the narrow doorway.

"Come, let me in!" he said gayly. "It's a cold night. You didn't expect me, did you, Mother Robb?"

"Dear me, what is it?" she faltered, stepping back as he came in, and dropping her crutch. "Be I dreamin'? I was a-dreamin' about — Oh, there! What was I a-sayin'? 'T ain't true! No! I've made some kind of a mistake."

Yes, and this was the man who kept the poorhouse, and she would go without complaint; they might have given her notice, but she must not fret.

"Sit down, sir," she said, turning toward him with touching patience. "You'll have to give me a little time. If I'd been notified I wouldn't have kept you waiting a minute this stormy night."

It was not the keeper of the poorhouse. The man by the door took one step forward and put his arm round her and kissed her.

"What are you talking about?" said John Harris. "You ain't goin' to make me feel like a stranger? I've come all the way from Dakota to spend Thanksgivin'. There's all sorts o' things out here in the wagon, an' a man to help get 'em in. Why, don't cry so, Mother Robb. I thought you'd have a great laugh, if I come and surprised you. Don't you remember I always said I should come?"

It was John Harris, indeed. The poor soul could say nothing. She felt now as if her heart was going to break with joy. He left her in the rocking-chair and came and went in his old boyish way, bringing in the store of gifts and provisions. It was better than any dream. He laughed and talked, and went out to send away the man to bring a wagonful of wood from John Mander's, and came in himself laden with pieces of the nearest fence to keep the fire going in the mean time. They must cook the beefsteak for supper right away; they must find the pound of tea among all the other bundles; they must get good fires started in both the cold bedrooms. Why, Mother Robb did n't seem to be ready for company from out West! The great, cheerful fellow hurried about the tiny house, and the little old woman limped after him, forgetting everything but hospitality. Had not she a house for John to come to? Were not her old chairs and tables in their places still? And he remembered everything, and kissed her as they stood before the fire, as if she were a girl.

He had found plenty of hard times, but luck had come at last. He had struck luck, and this was the end of a great year.

"No, I could n't seem to write letters; no use to complain o' the worst, an' I wanted to tell you the best when I came;" and he told it while she cooked the supper. "No, I wa'n't goin' to write no foolish letters," John repeated. He was afraid he should cry himself when he found out how bad things had been; and they sat down to supper together, just as they used to do when he was a homeless orphan boy, whom nobody else wanted in winter weather while he was crippled and could not work. She could not be kinder now than she was then, but she looked so poor and old! He saw her taste her cup of tea and set it down again with a trembling hand and a look at him. "No, I wanted to come myself," he blustered, wiping his eyes and trying to laugh. "And you're going to have everything you need to make you comfortable long's you live, Mother Robb!"

She looked at him again and nodded, but she did not even try to speak. There was a good hot supper ready, and a happy guest had come; it was the night before Thanksgiving.